LAW OF THE LAWLESS

Wayne C. Lee

Chivers Press
Bath, England

G.K. Hall & Co.
Thorndike, Maine USA

This Large Print edition is published by Chivers Press, England, and by G.K. Hall & Co., USA.

Published in 1999 in the U.K. by arrangement with Golden West Literary Agency.

Published in 1999 in the U.S. by arrangement with Golden West Literary Agency.

U.K. Hardcover ISBN 0–7540–3653–7 (Chivers Large Print)
U.K. Softcover ISBN 0–7540–3654–5 (Camden Large Print)
U.S. Softcover ISBN 0–7838–0442–3 (Nightingale Series Edition)

The text of this Large Print edition is unabridged.
Other aspects of the book may vary from the original edition.

Set in 16 pt. New Times Roman.

Printed in Great Britain on acid-free paper.

British Library Cataloguing in Publication Data available

Library of Congress Cataloging-in-Publication Data

Lee, Wayne C.
Law of the lawless / by Wayne C. Lee.
p. cm.
ISBN 0–7838–0442–3 (lg. print : sc : alk. paper)
1. Large type books. I. Title.
[PS3523.E34457L38 1999]
813'.54—dc21 98–48524

CHAPTER ONE

Dust sifted into the coach from the horses' hoofs and from the wheels churning up the dry powder in the road. None of the four passengers made any effort to beat it off their clothes.

Wade Tillotson sat beside a sullen dark-faced man who had barely spoken since Wade got on back at Blue Springs. Across from them sat two women. Wade already knew they were the Prandalls, mother and daughter, from Nevermore. He might not have paid as much attention to their had it not been for their destination.

'Is Nevermore much of a town?' he asked, fanning his hand at a fly that persisted in buzzing around his face.

'Not what it used to be,' Mrs. Prandall said. 'There are several vacant places now. Are you going to Nevermore?'

Wade nodded. 'I bought some land along Nevermore Creek from my cousin. She and her husband lived there. He was killed just recently.'

Wade was aware that both Mrs. Prandall and her daughter, Sue, had suddenly lost their listessness and were leaning forward, watching him. The silent man beside him had turned his head until his beady eyes were fastened on him, too.

'His name wasn't Runyan, was it?' Mrs. Prandall asked.

Wade nodded. 'That's right. Brent Runyan was my cousin's husband. Do you know anything about his death?'

Mrs. Prandall's lips pressed together and she shook her head. Her daughter was not so reluctant to speak.

'I'll bet Jasper Dovel could tell you,' she said.

'Be quiet, Sue,' her mother said. 'You've been away at school. You don't know what has been going on at home.'

'I know Mr. Dovel,' Sue said. 'He has run everything around Nevermore ever since I can remember. Before I left for school, he was swearing he'd get rid of every homesteader in the valley.'

'Hush, Sue,' Mrs. Prandall said sharply.

'Let her talk,' Wade said. 'I'm interested. My cousin told me a lot about Jasper Dovel and the Crudup brothers. I can't find out too much about them if I'm going to live there.'

'You'll be walking into a death trap,' Mrs. Prandall said, her face grim. 'What happened to Brent Runyan ought to tell you that.'

'I intend to find out what really did happen to him,' Wade said. 'I wrote to the town marshal, Deuce Ulrich, but he didn't answer.'

Wade was aware that the stranger beside him was listening intently to everything that was said even though he was pretending no interest now. There was no such pretense on the part of Mrs. Prandall and her daughter.

'You didn't tell Deuce you were coming to Nevermore, did you?' Mrs. Prandall asked.

Wade nodded. 'Of course. I'm a deputy U.S. marshal and I intend to look into Brent Runyan's death officially. I'll need the help of the local law officer.'

Mrs. Prandall shook her head and glanced nervously out the coach window. 'Like I said, Mr. Tillotson, you're walking right into a death trap. Deuce Ulrich is Jasper Dovel's tool. Deuce is the only law we have in Nevermore but he does exactly what Mr. Dovel tells him to.'

'No wonder I didn't get an answer,' Wade said.

'They're probably waiting to give you an answer when you get there,' Sue said.

'Doesn't sound like you have much law around Nevermore,' Wade said.

'The only law is Jasper Dovel's law,' Mrs. Prandall admitted. 'Before Jim Peterson gave up his homestead and left, he called that the law of the lawless.'

Wade was silent while the stage rolled dustily over another quarter of a mile. He remembered that the Claymore County sheriff, Ike Yancey, back in Blue Springs had warned him not to reveal his identity or plans. But Wade had been a deputy U. S. marshal for two years and he had never gained anything in an investigation by hiding his identity. In fact, letting people know he was a marshal had helped him solve a couple of cases.

Now he began to wonder if Sheriff Yancey had been right. After all, the sheriff was in control of the county right next to the one which claimed Nevermore within its boundaries.

'My cousin seemed to think that the Crudup brothers might have been responsible for Brent's death,' Wade said finally, breaking the silence.

'Tank and Hobie Crudup are as mean as sin,' Mrs. Prandall said, 'But they answer to Jasper Dovel, same as everyone else. Kate Crudup, their mother, is Jasper's sister. They came there at Jasper's invitation after Sam Crudup got himself killed down in Texas and left Kate a widow. They're as mean as Jasper, but they're not the boss.'

The stage started to slow down and Wade stuck his head out the window. A station was just ahead and Wade could see the stationmaster bringing a fresh team from the corral, harnessed and ready to go.

Wade let his eyes run over the station. This was the last one, according to the stage driver, before they reached Nevermore. After listening to Mrs. Prandall's repeated warning that he was riding into a death trap, his suspicions were growing by leaps and bounds.

What better place to spring the trap than at the last stage stop before Nevermore?

He tried to remember if he had told Ulrich just when he would be coming to Nevermore. He couldn't be sure that he had but he couldn't be sure that he hadn't, either. If the Crudup brothers and Jasper Dovel were as determined and as cold blooded as Mrs. Prandall described them, they might decide it would be better if he never got to Nevermore.

Wade shot a glance at the stranger beside him, wishing he knew who he was and where he was going. He'd failed to conceal his interest in what Mrs. Prandall had been saying. But Wade admitted he'd have had the same interest if he'd just been passing through the country. Trouble always attracted a man. Right now the stranger was staring ahead as if he, too, suspected there might be an ambush waiting and he wanted no part of it.

'I'd get off here and rent a horse to ride to Nevermore if I were you,' Mrs. Prandall said.

'You think they might try to take me off the stage?' Wade asked in surprise.

'If they know you're coming, there's no telling what they might do. I just don't want to see another killing. My husband is only half a man any more, he's that scared of Jasper Dovel and the Crudups.'

'Are they bothering you folks, too?'

Mrs. Prandall shook her head. 'They never bother us because we do exactly what they tell us to. And we'll keep on doing it. I shouldn't be telling you this, I reckon, but I'm hoping you'll show some sense and either turn around and go back or take a roundabout way to town. You might avoid being killed that way.'

The stage came to a stop and the driver jumped down to help the stationmaster change the team. The stranger opened the door and got out cautiously. Wade followed suit, helping Mrs. Prandall and her daughter down so they could walk around and stretch stiffened muscles.

Wade's eyes darted around the station, the barn, and corrals. Nothing seemed amiss and he concluded that there was nothing wrong. If this had been a trap, it would have been sprung before now.

'Are you going on to Nevermore on the stage?' Sue asked Wade fearfully.

'I reckon,' Wade said. 'My ticket is paid that far. It's hard to believe anyone would hold up a stage just to get a passenger. There are so many easier ways to get to a man than that.'

'We just might stay here until the next stage comes,' Mrs. Prandall said.

'Next stage won't be for two days,' the stationmaster said. 'I reckon me and my woman can put you up, though, if you're a mind to stay.'

'Pa will be worried if we don't come today,' Sue said.

'Reckon he would,' Mrs. Prandall agreed.

She sighed. 'Anyway, if they should decide to grab Mr. Tillotson, they wouldn't bother any of the rest of us.'

The team was hitched to the stage when Mrs. Prandall joined the driver and the stationmaster in an animated discussion but Wade couldn't hear what was being said. The stranger was prowling around the station yard like a cat on the hunt. Wade noted the tied-down holster, the soft step, the darting eyes. He had encountered gunmen before and this man fitted the description of a hired killer, not a man who killed on impulse.

'We'd better roll,' the driver shouted. Then he glared at Wade. 'You figure on going, too?'

'I bought my ticket to Nevermore,' Wade said.

'It could be to eternity,' the driver muttered and climbed up to the high seat.

Wade got into the coach, frowning. First it was Mrs. Prandall; now the stage driver. There could be no doubt that they were both afraid to have him aboard. Wade had originally had no doubts about the right way to approach his job here—come in openly with a show of law. Always before, that had brought the decent people to his side and he'd had little trouble ferreting out the lawbreaker he wanted. But he was not sure that was going to work in Nevermore. From Mrs. Prandall and the stage driver, he got the feeling that the law-abiding citizens of Nevermore would do nothing to help him. They would just try to keep out of his way so they wouldn't get involved in the showdown that was bound to come.

'What's the stage driver so upset about?' Wade asked as the coach moved out of the station yard.

'Mr. Skarsten just told me that he knows you wrote to Deuce Ulrich that you were coming,' Mrs. Prandall said. 'He thinks the same way I do—that Jasper Dovel may try to keep you from getting to Nevermore.'

'Maybe I should get out and walk,' Wade said testily.

'I don't reckon they'll hurt anybody but you. Only thing is, Herman Skarsten is not one to give up a passenger without a fight and he knows that fighting against Dovel or the Crudups isn't healthy.'

'He hadn't ought to fight,' the stranger said, speaking for one of the few times since Wade had boarded the stage. 'Ain't no skin off the driver's nose if they drag a passenger out and ventilate him.'

Mrs. Prandall looked at the stranger in disgust. 'Herman figures it's his duty to protect his passengers and cargo.'

The stranger shrugged and turned to stare out the window. 'If he wants to be a hero, that's his business.'

The stage gathered speed as it left the station behind and followed the south bank of Nevermore Creek. Silence settled down inside the coach but Wade felt the tension growing with each mile that fell behind. He caught himself scanning the prairie to the south and the low bluffs across the creek to the north.

Wade guessed they must be getting close to Nevermore when the team began laboring up a grade and he saw that they were on a high bluff that rose directly above the creek. The bluff on the north side of the river stood back half a mile from the stream and was little more than a gentle slope. The creek itself ran so close to the south bluff that Wade couldn't even see it from the coach window.

Wade saw the riders' come out of a draw to the southwest and head directly for the road, aiming at a spot that would intercept the stage. The stranger saw them, too, but he gave little outward indication of concern. Sue Prandall, sitting near the window on the south side, keeping an eye on the horizon, saw them and nudged her mother, who learned over Sue's lap to look.

'I knew it,' Mrs. Prandall said softly.

Wade already had his gun out of its holster and lying across his lap. 'Do you know them, ma'am?'

Mrs. Prandall started at the three riders a moment longer. As they came closer, Wade could see that they had masks across the lower parts of their faces.

'I know them, all right,' Mrs. Prandall said. 'I don't know why they are trying to hide their faces. Anybody in this country would know that big fat one is Tank Crudup. The one next to him, taller but not so fat, is his brother, Hobie. The other one looks like Luke Edris, their hired gunslinger. You'll see now why I said that you should have rented a horse to ride to Nevermore.'

Wade gripped his gun as the riders cut off the stage and the driver reined up.

'Just let my cargo be,' Herman Skarsten shouted. 'Stage robbing will get you in dutch, Tank. The company will have the law on your trail.'

'Keep your mouth shut!' the big rider said. 'We want a passenger you've got. How many are riding today?'

'Four,' Skarsten said. 'You'd better forget it, Tank.'

'You're too familiar with names,' the tall rider said. 'We don't like that.'

'Afraid somebody will identify you, Hobie?' Skarsten said.

'Let's get it over with,' the third rider put in.

Wade lifted his gun but Mrs. Prandall grabbed his arm. 'If you shoot just once, we'll all be dead in ten seconds,' she snapped. 'They're killers.'

'Jasper Dovel's orders, I suppose,' Wade said.

'Maybe,' Mrs. Prandall said. 'And maybe they're doing this on their own. The Crudups are bullheaded boys. I reckon if they weren't old Jasper's nephews, he'd have kicked their tails off his range long before this.'

The stranger now took his gun out and held it ready. The odds against them didn't seem insurmountable to Wade, but still he waited. Maybe Herman Skarsten could talk some sense into the Crudups. Wade had to give him a chance.

'You're a little free with your names, Skarsten,' the big rider said. 'Now I reckon we'll have to do something about you and everybody on your stage.'

Wade couldn't see what move Skarsten made, but he apparently reached for his rifle leaning against the dashboard at his feet. It was Hobie, the tall one, who shot him. Both Wade and the stranger shoved their guns through the window. But before they could fire, the stage lurched forward, the team frightened by the shot.

The stage careened off the road and hit some rocks on the top of the bluff. Wade fired anyway, hoping to be lucky. But the coach was bouncing so much, his gun seemed to be aimed either at the ground or the sky. The raiders fired some shots into the coach but, so far as Wade could see, they didn't hit anybody.

The team, apparently driverless, was running wildly now, moving back toward the road. The three riders pushed over against the four horses, crowding them toward the lip of the bluff. Mrs. Prandall and her daughter both screamed as they saw what was happening. The stranger cursed and fired his gun at the three men until it was empty. Wade, on the side away from the riders, fired any time he felt he had the remotest chance of hitting one of the men. But he couldn't see that either he or the stranger had scored.

Then suddenly one of the horses screamed in terror and the next instant the coach lurched to the right as the front wheel went over the bluff. The coach twisted and Wade saw the horses struggling frantically to get footing on the bluff. But two were already over and they dragged the other two after them.

It seemed to Wade that everything happened then in agonizingly slow motion. He was slammed against the top of the coach as it turned over. The door popped open and he was thrown toward it. He clawed frantically for anything to hang on to, but he couldn't stop himself.

Hurtling through the open door, he got a glimpse of the space below him and he realized it was much farther to the bottom of the bluff than he had thought.

He was aware of the coach tumbling beside him and of the horses, feet flaying, falling just below. Then he hit an outcropping on the bluff and was hurled farther out into space. Lights exploded in his head. The last sensation he had was of falling.

CHAPTER TWO

Everything was eerily quiet when Wade became aware of a sense of pain. His first realization was that he was still alive; that was followed by a feeling that it didn't matter. Like a total outsider observing an unimportant event, he thought that it would be better if he were dead.

Reality crept back to him with the searing pain in his head. Consciousness made him realize it was a miracle that he was alive. Those water willows where he had landed must have broken his fall.

He tried to move a hand and was almost surprised to find that he could. He tested each arm and leg, fighting to concentrate on what he was doing. If he let his mind wander, he had the feeling it would leave him entirely.

His thoughts sharpened suddenly when he remembered the wreck. Those men who had crowded the stagecoach off the road and over the bluff had been trying to kill him.

With a shock, he realized that everyone on that stage had gone over the bluff, too. If he hadn't been on the coach, those masked men wouldn't have wrecked it. Or would they? They hadn't even bothered to look inside the coach before sending it plunging over the bluff, so they might have wrecked it even if he had gotten off back at that last station.

Wade's head was splitting. He remembered being thrown out of the coach as it tumbled down the bluff. Apparently his head had hit a rock somewhere on the way down.

He tried moving and found that he could get up on his hands and knees. When he tried to stand, however, his knees buckled, the world spun, and he fell back to his knees. Looking at the wrecked coach, he knew he had to get over there and see if he could do anything for the passengers.

He began crawling painfully toward the coach, lying in the edge of the creek. Each move seemed to be tearing him apart. He discovered he had bruises all over, but no bones seemed to be broken. What about the other passengers? He didn't see any stir near the smashed vehicle.

If it wasn't for his throbbing head, Wade was sure he could get up and walk. His ribs felt as if half of them were broken but when he examined them tenderly, he concluded that they. were just badly bruised. Hardly any spot on his body had escaped some degree of injury.

As he crawled past some little water willows into an open meadow, his eyes swept up to the top of the bluff. Wade didn't know how long he had been unconscious; he had no sense of time having passed. He half expected to see the Crudups on the bluff, making sure no one had survived the crash. But the skyline was empty.

Apparently the Crudups had decided everyone on the coach had been killed and there was no need to come down to verify it.

The thought pushed Wade harder as he crawled toward the coach. He knew they had been after him. Deuce Ulrich must have told Dovel that he was coming to Nevermore. Wade's cousin had warned Wade to watch out for Jasper Dovel and the Crudups, but she hadn't mentioned Ulrich. Hadn't she known that he was Dovel's man?

Wade crawled as fast as he could toward the coach. It was quite a distance from the place where he had landed. He must have bounced off at an angle when he hit those rocks. The only movement he saw near the coach was one horse struggling feebly. The others seemed to be dead.

The first passenger he reached was Sue Prandall. She was ten feet from the coach and he knew before he touched her that she was dead. Her head was cocked at a weird angle. A broken neck. It could have happened as she bounced around inside the coach as it crashed down the side of the bluff or it could have snapped when she was thrown out of the coach, apparently on impact with the ground at the foot of the bluff.

Wade moved on. Near the coach he found Mrs. Prandall. He felt her wrist. There was no pulse. Her body was still warm. That gave him a clue as to how long he had been unconscious.

It didn't look to him as if Mrs. Prandall had moved since coming to rest where she was now.

Only a few feet from Mrs. Prandall was Herman Skarsten, the stage driver. A bullet hole in the chest showed how he had died. If he had not been dead, he probably would have kept the team from going over the bluff.

There was one more to find, the quiet stranger who had sat beside Wade. He was nowhere in sight. Wade crawled on, his stomach churning at the sight of those who had been his traveling companions so recently.

Crawling to the coach, he went around behind it. There he found the stranger, pinned beneath one of the big wheels of the coach. Wade couldn't tell whether the tumble down the bluff had killed him, or if he had been crushed beneath the heavy wheel. He certainly had not suffered any more after that wheel came to rest on him.

Wade moved closer. He knew the identity of the other people on the coach. But he still had no idea who the stranger was. Surely he was carrying some papers that would identify him.

His body was in the edge of the creek but his gun had landed ten feet away, up on the creek bank. Wade realized he had lost his own gun in the fall, and he certainly didn't feel like crawling around looking for it. He also knew that if those men wanted him dead so much that they would run the coach off the bluff to kill everyone on it just to get him, they wouldn't hesitate to kill him on sight if they found him alive now. He had to have a gun.

His first move was to crawl to the gun and shove it into his own holster. Then he moved over to the stranger's body and began going through his pockets. He found a roll of bills, but he put it back. He had no intention of robbing the dead.

Finally, in an inside coat pocket, he found what he was looking for; a letter addressed to Wade Vaun. He took the letter out of the envelope and glanced over it. It was from some girl down in Dodge City, but it added nothing about the identity of Wade Vaun. The letter carried three mark-ups of addresses. Apparently Wade Vaun moved around quite a bit.

Wade's eyes went to the top of the bluff again. The skyline was still empty. In spite of his splitting head, Wade felt the danger. If one of the Crudups returned to check on the wreck and saw movement down here, he'd come down immediately and investigate. The one the Crudups wanted dead most of all was still alive. But he wouldn't be for long if they saw him.

Suddenly an idea broke through the pain in his throbbing head. The stranger had the same first name that he had. If he could suddenly become Wade Vaun instead of Wade Tillotson, he would be a lot safer. He had no idea who

Wade Vaun was or where he had been going. But whoever he was, Wade Vaun was sure to be safer around Nevermore than Wade Tillotson. What the Crudups had done to try to get rid of Marshal Wade Tillotson was proof of that.

Wade went through his own pockets carefully, taking out everything that would identify him as Wade Tillotson. Then he just as carefully went through the pockets of the dead man, removing all evidence that he was Wade Vaun. There was very little to remove. Apparently Vaun had not been eager for people to know who he was.

Carefully then Wade placed his own identification, including his deputy marshal's badge, on the dead man and took the letter he had found on Vaun and put it in his own pocket. It wasn't a very savory thing to carry around, but it would proclaim him to be Wade Vaun, not Wade Tillotson. That was all that mattered at the moment.

Identitied now as Wade Vaun, Wade turned back toward the willows growing along the creek beyond the meadow. His headache was worse, if that was possible. At times he felt that he was going to pass out right where he was. He didn't want to be found out here in the meadow. Someone would surely come looking for the stage soon, and Wade needed time to collect his thoughts and do some planning before he had to explain who he was and why he was here.

He crawled on toward the willows, worrying that he wasn't going to make it. Just the thought of standing on his feet made his head reel.

He had to stop for breath several times before reaching the willows, and when he finally got to them, he glanced back and was dismayed at how close to the wrecked stage he was even yet. He crawled farther into the willows. There, with the little willows forming a canopy over his head, he stretched out with a groan.

The ground was damp so close to the river, but Wade was past caring if his bed was dry. His head throbbed until he saw lights flashing in front of his eyes with every heart beat. He tried to relax and almost immediately felt himself slipping away.

It was the sound of a shot that brought Wade out of the depths again. The sun had passed its zenith and was slanting down on him, putting some light in his face through the twigs of the willows.

His mind came alert as he realized that had really been a shot he had heard and not a dream. He shifted enough to see through the willows, wincing and almost crying out with the pain. But he could see.

There were four men out there at the wreck, moving around slowly, talking in subdued tones as men do in the presence of death. One man had just put the crippled horse out of its misery.

'Who's going to tell George Prandall?' one of the men asked, the first words that Wade understood.

'I'd rather be shot than do it,' another man said. 'George's whole life was wrapped up in Nancy and Sue.'

'It's going to be hard on Effie, too,' another man said. 'Herman was the only family she had.'

Wade realized this man was talking about the stage driver, Herman Skarsten. Effie must be his wife or daughter.

Wade shifted his position until he could see better. One man had found the body of the gunman now. His voice rose a little as he announced his discovery.

'Here's a man pinned under the wheel. Never saw him before.'

The other men hurried over and there was a buzz of low voices that Wade couldn't understand. Then three men lifted the wheel of the stage just enough so that the fourth man could drag the body out from under it.

'Bring the wagon,' the man said. 'We'll take the bodies in.'

While one man went for the wagon, another went through the pockets of the stranger. 'Here's who this fellow is. Wade Tillotson. And look here. A deputy marshal's badge. Suppose he could have been coming here to investigate some of these killings?'

'Probably Brent Runyan's murder,' another man said. 'Mrs. Runyan said she had a cousin who was a marshal, and she was going to have him come and find the man who killed her husband.'

'If that's who he was, he's better off dead now than later,' the first man said. 'He sure wouldn't have arrested anybody around Nevermore and gotten away with it.'

'Reckon that's right. Maybe this wreck happened because of him.'

'You mean this was planned?'

'Did you ever hear of a team deliberately running off a bluff?'

'Hey,' another man called. 'Look here. Herman was shot.'

Wade realized that the men had made such a quick initial examination that they had missed the bullet hole in Herman Skarsten's chest.

'Guess that answers your question. Somebody shot Herman then crowded the stage off the bluff. Killed four people just to get rid of one. Who would do a thing like that?'

'Do you have to ask?' another man grunted angrily. 'Especially if they knew there was a marshal on board.'

The wagon rumbled up and the men loaded the four bodies. Then three of the men went to some horses standing back a ways from the wreck while the fourth one drove the wagon. Within a couple of minutes they had disappeared upstream, apparently heading for the town of Nevermore.

Wade waited until the sound of their movements had faded then crawled out of the willows again. His head felt better, but it was still aching fiercely. He was more aware of the dozens of other bruises he had now. He had to find a place where he could climb the bluff to the stage road and head back for the station where they had stopped earlier this morning.

He wouldn't abandon the idea of coming to Nevermore and arresting the man who had killed Brent Runyan, but he was in no shape right now to do any investigating, much less arrest the man and get him out of the country. He also had some others now to bring to justice. Four innocent people had been murdered today, and Wade knew the men who were responsible. He wouldn't rest easy until he had brought the Crudups to trial.

Once out of the willows, Wade got slowly to his feet. He swayed back and forth like a twig in a high wind, but he managed to stay upright. His head cleared a little and he examined himself once more. He couldn't find any broken bones but he was a mass of very sore bruises.

Moving slowly, he reached the creek and waded across. It wasn't more than four inches deep. At the foot of the bluff, he began searching for a way to climb to the top. There was no possibility at the spot where the stage had gone over. That was almost a straight wall. Glancing up and down the river, it appeared that the bluff was lower upstream, while it loomed up high as far as he could see the other way. He didn't want to get any closer to Nevermore, but his foggy mind was obsessed with the necessity of getting up to that road.

Turning upstream, he hurried along as fast as his aching bones and muscles would take him. He had to get out of the vicinity of the wreck because he knew that as soon as the people in town learned about it, curiosity would bring a great many of them down here to see it.

Finding a place where the wall was not so steep, Wade started climbing. It was slow going, and he was short of both breath and strength. After ten minutes, he paused and looked down. He was only a few feet off the valley floor. At this rate, he would never get to the top.

His strength was about gone. He realized that he couldn't climb out tonight. He had better find a place to rest through the night and try it again in the morning.

Cautiously he backed down to the valley floor, taking only a minute to cover the distance he had used ten minutes climbing. He found a fence in his way as he sought cover in some bigger willows he saw nearby. Climbing through the fence, he dragged himself across the meadow to the trees.

The trees offered good protection from prying eyes, but little from the coolness of the night that would hit him soon. There wasn't anything he could do about that.

As soon as he sank to the ground, a great weariness washed over him. He knew he was passing out again, but he didn't care any more.

He didn't know how long he was unconscious this time, but when he came out of the fog, he became aware of sounds nearby and he realized he had been discovered.

CHAPTER THREE

Wade's first reaction was to reach for his gun. He knew he'd be no match for a man who was hunting for him. But he had to try. He had little use for a man who didn't make an effort to defend himself.

A gasp stopped him. It was not the sound of someone planning to kill him. He blinked his eyes against the sinking sun. Then he saw a woman staring down at him. When she moved a little to one side where the sun wasn't directly behind her, he saw that she was young, little more than a girl—probably eighteen or twenty. She might be a young rancher's wife.

'Who are you?' she demanded.

Wade tried to talk and discovered that his tongue was so sore and thick that he couldn't form any words. He must have bitten it severely when he fell. The girl apparently saw then how battered and bruised he was, for her eyes widened even more.

'How did you get here?' she asked.

Again Wade tried to answer but all he could manage was a mumble. He had some questions of his own he'd like to ask, but they'd have to wait until the swelling went out off his tongue so he could talk.

The girl stared down at Wade. 'You can't talk, can you?'

He shook his head.

'Are you hurt bad?'

He nodded. There was no point in denying it. He watched her as she studied him, apparently trying to decide what she should do.

'You're in our pasture,' she said finally. 'I came down to find our milk cows. I'll get Pa to bring a wagon and haul you up to the house. Ma can fix you up.'

All he could do was nod his appreciation. He didn't know who she was. He would rather have slipped out of the country without anyone knowing he was even here, but a little doctoring of his bruises would likely get him on his feet a lot quicker.

The girl disappeared and Wade stared after her. She evidently was not anybody's wife. She had spoken of Pa and Ma, not her husband.

She must be a homesteader's daughter. It wasn't likely that a ranch girl would be looking for milk cows. From what Wade's cousin had said, the Dovels and the Crudups had driven out most of the homesteaders around Nevermore. Brent Runyan had been among the last to hang on. The girl could belong to a family that worked for Jasper Dovel and were permitted a small place with a couple of milk cows.

The sun was down when Wade heard the rumble of a wagon. He waited, wondering what he would see. Would it be some stubborn homesteader who had refused to yield to the pressure of Jasper Dovel and the Crudups? Or would it be one of their stooges? Wade was glad that he had gotten rid of everything that would identify him as Wade Tillotson, the deputy marshal.

The homesteader who climbed down from the wagon and walked over to stare down at Wade was a square-built man of average height and more than average weight. He hitched up his overalls as if that would make the pouch in front of him disappear.

'Looks like you've had a rough time, fellow,' he said. 'Come on, Cozetta, give me a hand in getting him in the wagon.'

Wade had been so interested in the homesteader that he hadn't noticed that the girl had come back with her father. There was little resemblance between the two, he saw.

The girl had blue eyes and long blond hair hanging in braids down her back. Her father had brown straggly hair showing under his old cap, and brown watery eyes.

Wade bit his lip to keep from yelling when they moved him. He realized that he wouldn't have been able to move at all by morning if he had lain here on the damp ground all night. He wouldn't have moved right now if he had any choice, but he didn't. The man's hands were rough but somehow gentle, as if he'd handled injured things before.

The girl had spread some blankets in the bed of the wagon and Wade was laid on them. He didn't object to their treating him like a helpless invalid, which he wasn't far from being right now. The bruises had tightened up his muscles until moving any of them was torture.

Cozetta sat near Wade and rolled a corner of the blanket into a pillow beneath his head as the man clucked to the team and turned the wagon back the way it had come. Wade was sure the jolt of the wagon would tear him apart, but he pinched his lips together and held back the groans.

It seemed like the wagon bumped along forever before the man halted the team. By then, the sheer pleasure of the cessation of movement overshadowed any concern about where he was. But the peace of lying still was soon destroyed by the man who came around to the back of the wagon.

'Help me get him out, Cozetta,' he said. 'Ruth will have a place ready for him.'

Cozetta made the moving as easy as possible until the man got him out of the wagon. Then he picked him up like a big rag doll and carried him into the house, Cozetta running ahead to open the door. A women met them and directed her husband to a cot at one end of the living room. She was just a little shorter than Cozetta, and heavier, although she appeared slim compared to her husband.

Cozetta pulled Wade's boots off, but no one made any attempt to get him out of his other clothes. The woman quickly examined him by the light of a lamp Cozetta held.

'Don't seem to be any bones broken,' the woman said. She looked at Wade's face. 'You look something like a piece of well-pounded beefsteak ready for the frying pan. Who beat you up?'

Wade tried to answer but again found he could only mumble unintelligibly.

'He can't talk, Ma,' Cozetta said. 'I asked him some questions before we brought him in. All he did was mumble.'

'I want to know who he is,' the man said gruffly, glaring down at Wade.

'He probably wants to know who we are, too,' the woman said. She looked at Wade. 'Can you understand us?'

Wade nodded.

'I'm Ruth Burdeen,' the woman said. 'My

husband, Amos, and my daughter, Cozetta, brought you here. We own this little farm close to Nevermore. Did you have a horse? Did he fall with you?'

Wade shook his head.

'Let's find out who he is,' Amos Burdeen said. 'Then we'll have a better idea how he got into our pasture.'

With rough hands, Amos went through Wade's pockets. When he found the envelope addressed to Wade Vaun, he held it up to the light and stared at it.

'Wade Vaun,' he said as though the words were a curse. He turned and glared at Wade. 'You were on that stage today, weren't you?'

Wade nodded, wondering why the name of Wade Vaun had brought such a scowl to Amos Burdeen's face. But no matter who Vaun was, it had to be better than letting people know he was Wade Tillotson, the deputy marshal.

'What about the stage, Amos?' Mrs. Burdeen asked. 'Did you hear something about it in town?'

Amos looked at his wife and daughter then jerked his head toward the kitchen. They followed him through the partition door and Wade could hear Amos's voice rumbling in there. He apparently had heard about the stage wreck, but hadn't told his family yet.

But that didn't explain why the name of Vaun had turned Amos's tentative welcome to a scowl. Wade didn't need to be told now that he wasn't welcome in Amos Burdeen's house. Now he had to find out why. Who was Wade Vaun, and what had he let himself in for by taking his identity?

After a long time Cozetta came back into the room where Wade was lying. She brought a bowl of thin soup and insisted on feeding him, even though he tried to make her believe he could do it himself.

She didn't say anything, but he felt the coolness in her and he could see from the redness of her eyes that she had been crying. That called for an explanation, but he knew he wasn't going to get one. He was sure he was being blamed for whatever had made her cry. As soon as he could control this thick tongue of his, he'd get some answers some way.

When the soup was gone, Cozetta went back into the kitchen and none of the family showed up again until they passed through the room on their way to their bedrooms. Amos was the only one to look at him and he gave him a dark scowl.

Wade slept only a little during the night. He was so sore that any move he made sent sharp pains ripping through him, yet he couldn't bear to remain in one position too long.

Morning came at last, and the three Burdeens passed back through the room to the kitchen. Cozetta stopped at his cot long enough to see that he was still alive. Wade felt that her concern was no deeper than that.

After half an hour she brought him some coffee and two soft fried eggs. She sat on a chair next to him and prepared to feed him.

'Can you talk yet?' she asked.

He tried. 'I guess so,' he said. His voice was husky and the words thick but understandable. 'I can feed myself, too.'

'You'll have to sit up if you're going to feed yourself,' Cozetta said.

Gritting his teeth against the pain of every move, Wade pushed his feet off the cot and to the floor and pulled himself to a sitting position. His head almost split and the room spun around, but he held himself upright by gripping the side of the cot with both hands.

Cozetta watched him closely for a minute.

'Maybe you're stronger than we thought. That's good. The sooner you can get on your way, the better.'

'I have the feeling I'm as welcome here as a polecat,' Wade said slowly. 'Mind telling me why?'

'You should know,' Cozetta said hotly. 'We're homesteaders, Mr. Vaun.'

Wade held his head with both hands. 'I must have taken an awful wallop on the head when I fell down that bluff. I can't seem to remember anything very well.'

'Maybe that fall knocked some sense into your head. Don't you even remember Jasper Dovel?'

Wade nodded. 'The name sounds familiar.'

'It should, seeing that he hired you to come here to be his killer.'

Wade caught his breath. The stranger in the coach yesterday hadn't said where he was going. It was the worst kind of luck that he had been coming to the same place as Wade. By switching identity with the stranger, Wade must have put himself on Jasper Dovel's side in the struggle here at Nevermore.

For a moment he considered telling Cozetta the truth. Then he canceled that idea. His only chance of survival, until he could take care of himself at least, was to keep his real identity hidden. Obviously the Burdeens didn't intend to kill him, although they considered him their enemy. If he was Wade Tillotson, the marshal, he wouldn't last any longer than a grasshopper in a prairie fire, if he fell into the hands of Jasper Dovel or the Crudups.

'Know anything else about me?' Wade asked finally.

'Apparently more than you know about yourself,' Cozetta said. 'I know that Tank and Hobie Crudup don't like the idea of Mr. Dovel hiring you.'

Wade frowned. 'It runs in my mind that Jasper Dovel and the Crudups were supposed to be on the same side.'

'You're remembering now,' Cozetta said icily. 'Kate Crudup is Jasper Dovel's sister. Mr. Dovel is the big dog around Nevermore. Always has been. But Tank and Hobie don't kowtow to him.'

'You seem to know a lot about them,' Wade said, trying to make his words clear but still feeling like he was talking around a mouthful of mush.

'She should,' Ruth Burdeen said as she came in from the kitchen in time to hear what Wade had said. 'She's been seeing Hobie Crudup quite often lately.'

'Ma,' Cozetta said, 'that's none of his business.'

'Shouldn't be yours, either,' Mrs. Burdeen said.

Wade sensed the anger in her voice. She obviously didn't approve of Cozetta's interest in Hobie Crudup. From what Wade had seen of the Crudups, he'd have to go along with Mrs. Burdeen's judgment.

'Pa says it's the only way we're going to get to stay here,' Cozetta said. 'Anyway, he's not so bad.'

'This place is our home,' Mrs. Burdeen said, 'but it's not worth that price.' She turned her attention to Wade. 'Now that you can talk, tell us what happened.'

'Some masked men held up the stage,' Wade said slowly, forming the words carefully. 'Shot the driver then crowded the team over the edge of the bluff.'

'That must have been Dovel's men,' Cozetta said quickly.

'You didn't recognize any of them?' Mrs.

Burdeen asked.

'I don't know anybody here,' Wade said.

'Your memory seems to be returning pretty well,' Cozetta said, looking at Wade suspiciously.

'I'm not liable to forget that tumble off the bluff,' Wade said.

'Why would Jasper have the stage wrecked without taking you off?' Mrs. Burdeen asked.

'Didn't he know you were coming on this stage?' Cozetta demanded.

Wade shook his head. 'I don't think so. My mind is still pretty foggy on some things.'

He was tempted to tell them it was the Crudups who had forced the coach over the edge of the bluff.

But he had the feeling that Cozetta was not too reluctant to follow her father's orders to keep company with Hobie Crudup. The less he said against the Crudups, the better off he'd be until he was able to get out of here. He wouldn't stay with the Burdeens any longer than absolutely necessary.

'Could have been Tank and Hobie who forced the stage over the bluff,' Mrs. Burdeen said. 'Jasper Dovel would have done it to get rid of that marshal. But maybe Tank and Hobie knew that Vaun was on that stage, too. They could kill two birds with one stone this way, then tell Jasper they were only after the marshal.'

'Ma, you've got a suspicious mind,' Cozetta

said.

'You notice whoever did it didn't try to save Nancy and Sue Prandall,' her mother reminded.

Tears welled into Cozetta's eyes. 'I could kill the men myself if I find out for sure who did that.' She looked at Wade. 'Sue was my best friend.'

'I'm sorry about both of them,' Wade said. 'They seemed very nice. The driver was shot only because he was trying to protect the passengers.'

Mrs. Burdeen nodded. 'That sounds like Herman Skarsten. I feel so sorry for Effie. She has no one left now.'

Wade had a lot of questions, but he felt the two Burdeen women had given him all the information he could expect. He ate his breakfast even though his mouth was so sore he could barely chew and the hot coffee seemed to scald it.

After the dishes had taken back to the kitchen, Wade did some hard thinking. One thing sure, he had to get out of here as quickly as possible. The longer he stayed here, the more danger he exposed the Burdeens to. If the Crudups were trying to get rid of Dovel's hired killer, they'd take out their fury on the Burdeens if they found them helping him.

Shortly before noon, Cozetta came hurrying into the room. 'You'll have to go back into the bedroom,' she said sharply. 'We have company.

Can you make it that far?'

'I reckon,' Wade said and got slowly off the cot. His head still seemed ready to burst and the room swayed before his eyes, but he managed to totter into the bedroom with Cozetta holding one arm.

Once inside the room, Cozetta led him to the bed where he sat down. Then she ran out and shut the door. He could hear her scurrying around the room, apparently gathering up all evidence that anyone had been lying on the cot there.

Wade wondered who was coming that the Burdeens didn't want to see him. He heard voices outside; then they came closer and he realized they were in the big room where he had been lying on the cot.

'I've been down to see the stage wreck,' a man's voice said. 'Really a mess.'

'First you'd seen it, Hobie?' Mrs. Burdeen asked suspiciously.

Hobie Crudup! Now Wade knew why he had been hustled out of sight.

'Yep,' Hobie said. 'Reckon Uncle Jasper was making sure that marshal didn't get to Nevermore. Too bad about the Prandalls getting killed in the wreck. I was talking to the man down at the last stage station. He said there were two men passengers on that stage. Wonder what happened to the other one?'

'I supposed the men from town found everybody,' Cozetta said.

‘They only found one man,’ Hobie said.

‘Nobody could have gone over that bluff in that coach and survived, the way I hear it,’ Mrs. Burdeen said.

‘Sure doesn’t seem like it,’ Hobie admitted. ‘But I looked around down there and I couldn’t find the other man. He must have crawled off somewhere to die.’

‘That doesn’t seem likely,’ Mrs. Burdeen said. ‘Anyway, if Jasper got the marshal, what does he care about the other man? He sure didn’t care about Herman Skarsten or Nancy and Sue Prandall.’

‘That other man could have been Jasper’s hired gun,’ Hobie said. ‘I’d just like to know what happened to him.’

Hobie went back outside. Half an hour later, Cozetta brought Wade’s dinner to him. Her eyes were still red and he could see that she’d been crying again.

‘We’re going to Nancy’s and Sue’s funeral this afternoon,’ she said. ‘You’ll be all right here alone.’

‘Sure,’ Wade said. ‘I can get around by myself now if I have to. I’ll leave as soon as I can.’ He heard them drive away in the wagon shortly after dinner. Wade got up from the bed and walked around slowly, getting the feel of his legs under him again. He wasn’t ready to go out on his own yet, but he must leave soon. Hobie might suspect that the Burdeens had found him. They apparently were the only ones who lived near the scene of the wreck and Hobie hadn't been able to find him.

As the afternoon wore along, Wade walked around the room several times. His strength was returning rapidly. His head still ached and his bruises were very painful, but exercise would help them.

Then he heard a horse in the yard and looked out. He recognized the tall rider as the man who had shot the stage driver, Hobie Crudup.

CHAPTER FOUR

Hobie had not ridden his horse up to the front of the house but had stopped out near the shed where he could not be seen from the front door of the house.

To Wade, that suggested that Hobie thought the missing man was hiding here at Burdeens' and he intended to sneak in and surprise him while the Burdeens were all at the funeral of Nancy and Sue Prandall.

Wade watched Hobie nudge his horse over behind the shed and a moment later he came around the corner on foot and moved toward the back of the house. Wade knew his chances were slim if Hobie found him.

He moved back from the window. He didn't need to watch Hobie any longer. It wasn't easy for Wade to move around yet, but he had to move now. He crossed to the bureau where Cozetta had laid his gun and belt. Lifting the gun from its holster, he remembered suddenly that this was Vaun's gun and it was empty. Vaun had fired every shot at the Crudups before the stagecoach went over the bluff. Quickly he punched out the empty cartridge and thumbed in fresh ones. Then he wobbled back to the chair that stood along one wall, almost behind the door, and flopped down on it. There he cocked the gun and aimed it at the door and waited.

Out in the other part of the house, he heard the creak of a floor board. Hobie was inside the house. He'd soon look here in this bedroom where Cozetta had told him to stay while they were gone to the funeral.

Wade was prepared when the door of the bedroom suddenly burst open and Hobie leaped inside, the gun in his hand aimed at the bed.

'Drop it or you're dead,' Wade said sharply.

Hobie started to turn toward the sound then checked himself, turning only his head. He looked at the gun in Wade's hand and saw that it was cocked.

'You're sick,' Hobie said after a long minute. 'I can still get you.'

'Want to try it?' Wade challenged. 'If you don't, drop your gun.'

Wade held the gun in both hands. He might

not be able to hold it steady enough to hit a vital spot, but the range was too close to miss entirely, and Hobie knew it. Slowly Hobie let his gun slip from his fingers. It chunked loudly in the silence as it hit the floor.

'You're Uncle Jasper's new gun hand, ain't you?' Hobie asked.

'You might call me that,' Wade said.

'You didn't think I intended to shoot you, did you?' Hobie asked, his voice wheedling now.

'Why else did you bang in here with your gun ready for action?'

'I figured you'd be nervous and I didn't want you shooting me before I had a chance to explain that Jasper Dovel is my uncle. We're on the same side. Now how about letting me pick up my gun?'

Wade shook his head. 'I didn't live this long being that thickheaded. When a man barges into a room with a gun in his hand, I figure he intends to use it. Now just what did you want?'

'To make sure you came through that wreck all right. I heard there were two men on that stage, and I figured one of them was the man Uncle Jasper had sent for. I only wanted to be sure you lived through it.'

'And make sure I didn't live long enough to tell about it if I did,' Wade added.

Hobie scowled at him. 'You are an unfriendly cuss,' he said.

'I don't take kindly to people trying to kill

me,' Wade said. 'Especially the second time. Now I reckon you'd better get out of here before I decide to pay you what I owe you for running that stage over the bluff.'

Hobie sighed. 'Uncle Jasper is going to be plenty mad when he finds out you're staying with a homesteader.' He started to stoop for his gun.

'Leave it there,' Wade said sharply. 'If you bring trouble on the people who have helped me, I swear I'll hunt you down like a dog and kill you.'

Hobie glared at Wade for a minute and apparently saw nothing to make him think Wade was bluffing. With an unintelligible grunt, he backed out the door and Wade heard him clumping across the floor to the outside.

Wade moved to the window and watched Hobie go to the shed and get his horse. Only after he had ridden out of sight along the river did Wade move. Hobie knew where he was now and he knew the Burdeens wouldn't be home until after the funeral. Wade couldn't even guess how long that would be. Hobie might come back, making sure this time that Wade didn't see him until he could strike.

Wade moved to the bureau and buckled on his gunbelt, dropping the gun into the holster. Amos had found his hat and brought it in last night and Wade got it now. Moving to the side of the house, he opened it carefully, looking around for any sign of Hobie. Everything was quiet.

Slipping outside, Wade hurried as fast as he could toward the creek. There were willows along the bank that would conceal him. Until he tried to run, he didn't realize just how much he still hurt. His fastest pace was a slow shuffle.

Once he reached the willows, he settled down out of sight and watched to see if Hobie appeared. He might have seen him leave the house. When he didn't show up in the next ten minutes, Wade began to relax. He hurt all over now. Another couple, of days in bed was what he needed. But there was no way he was going to get that. There was no doubt in Wade's mind now that Cozetta was right about the Crudups not wanting Jasper Dovel's gunman here. They must think they were capable of doing any gun work themselves.

Wade moved deeper into the willows and when he felt he was safely out of sight of anyone passing by, he nestled down near a small tree, keeping his gun in his hand.

The afternoon was warm and he dozed at times, waking up feeling stiff and sorer than before. But he knew the rest was doing him good even if the damp ground was not.

It was someone pushing through the willows that wakened him the last time. Gripping his gun tightly, he turned his eyes toward the sound and waited. It surely wasn't Hobie. He wouldn't make that much racket. Whoever was coming either didn't expect him to be here, or had no fear of him if he was.

The sound came closer and then he saw Cozetta moving through the willows, obviously looking for something, probably him.

'Over here,' he called softly. He lowered the gun in his lap as she approached.

'What happened to make you come out here?' she demanded when she reached him.

'I had company while you were gone. Hobie seemed intent on causing another funeral. When he left, I thought I'd better get out of the house before he came back.'

Cozetta didn't seem surprised. 'Hobie is suspicious. I was afraid we hadn't fooled him this morning. Our farm is the only one close to the place where the stage was wrecked. And Hobie knew there was another man on that stage.'

Wade almost said that he should have known, since he helped force it over the bluff. But he held back. Cozetta seemed to be attacted to Hobie and Wade couldn't afford to antagonize her now.

'Better come back to the house now,' she said. 'It will get cold out here tonight. Anyway, Hobie wouldn't really hurt you. He just wants you to get out of the country.'

'You could get in trouble if I'm found in your house,' Wade said.

'I doubt it,' Cozetta said. 'I can handle Hobie. And Jasper Dovel should appreciate the fact that we're keeping you alive, since he sent for you.'

Wade hadn't thought of it that way. Slowly he got to his feet and followed Cozetta out of the willows and back to the house.

'I don't think we'll see any of them tonight, anyway,' she said.

'I'm feeling well enough now I can take care of myself,' Wade said. 'I'll get out tomorrow—or tonight if you have any more visitors.'

Amos Burdeen was tight-lipped throughout the evening and Wade felt about as welcome in his house as the smallpox. Ruth Burdeen was more cordial and Cozetta treated him like a welcome guest. She was confident that his presence wouldn't cause trouble and explained to her father that showing kindness to Dovel's gunman should bring some consideration from Dovel.

Cozetta was right about the Burdeens' having no visitors that night. Wade woke the next morning feeling more like himself than he had since the wreck. Today he would leave here.

But he wasn't quick enough carrying out his resolve. Breakfast was barely over when Hobie rode into the yard, coming up to the hitchrail in front of the house this time.

Wade lost no time in grabbing up his few things and hurrying into the room from which the side door opened out toward the river. He paused there as Hobie knocked on the front door. He'd have to wait until Hobie was inside the house before he went outside. He doubted if he would make it to the willows if Hobie saw him.

He heard Cozetta invite Hobie inside. At first the voices were quiet, then they rose quickly.

'You stay out of there, Hobie.' That was Cozetta's voice over near the bedroom.

'You're hiding a gunman, Cozetta,' Hobie shouted. 'Maybe you don't know it, but he was brought here to kill your pa and burn you out. I aim to see that he doesn't get the job done.'

Wade didn't wait any longer. When Hobie didn't find him in the bedroom, he'd search the rest of the house. Wade intended to be out in the willows before then.

As he hurried into the willows, he wondered if Cozetta would believe that Wade had come to kill Amos Burdeen and run the rest of the family out of the valley. Wade didn't know whether or not Hobie was telling the truth. Maybe Jasper Dovel had sent for Wade Vaun to do just that.

As Wade hurried up the river bank in the direction he knew would take him to Nevermore, he tried to plan his next move. He certainly wasn't going to do Jasper Dovel's dirty work. He had come here to find the killer of Brent Runyan. When that was done, he intended to settle on the land he had bought from Brent Runyan's widow.

But right now he had to concentrate on surviving. He certainly wasn't going to make it if his real identity became known. Probably his best bet was to proceed with his masquerade. He'd go to Jasper Dovel's, pretending to be Wade Vaun. The Crudups obviously didn't know what Vaun looked like. Wade would have to gamble that Dovel didn't, either. Being in Jasper Dovel's house would not only offer Wade some security from the Crudups, but would also give him a chance to find out about Dovel's operations. That could be the fastest way to get to the truth of Brent Runyan's murder.

Wade was weak and his head still hurt, but the night's sleep had done a great deal for him. For the first time since the wreck, he felt that he could take care of himself. Still, he was about worn out when he reached the town of Nevermore.

The town was on the south side of the creek. Wade had come up the north bank of the creek, so he had to cross the wooden bridge at the north end of Main Street. The livery barn was the first building south of the bridge on the east side of the street and Wade turned in there.

In the office of the barn was a young man, little more than a fuzzy-cheeked boy, and an older man, whiskers bristling like an angry porcupine. Wade had to have a horse to get onto Dovel's ranch even if that was near town, and he had to find out where that road was.

Wade sized up the two and decided that the older man was the one who would know everybody here, although he doubted if there was anyone in Nevermore who didn't know where Jasper Dovel lived.

'Can you tell me how to get to Dovel's ranch?' Wade asked, leaning against the wall to rest.

The older man's eyes brightened like glowing coals. 'What do you want with old Jasper? Who are you?'

Wade eyed the old man with alarm. 'I've got business with him,' he said.

'You're that gunman he hired, ain't you?' the old man yelled. 'If I had a gun, I'd kill you right where you stand.'

'Hold on, old man,' Wade said, stepping out of the office doorway. 'I asked you a civil question.'

'What's civil about a man who comes here to kill us all?' the old man shouted, coming out into the alleyway of the barn.

'I'm not here to kill anybody,' Wade insisted. 'I want to know where Dovel lives.'

'You ain't denying you came here to do his dirty work, are you?'

'I came here to talk to him,' Wade said.

The old man suddenly lunged for a pitchfork that was leaning against the partition between two stalls. Wade reached for his gun but didn't draw it. He didn't want to shoot the old man, and he doubted if just the sight of the gun would stop him. He was insane. Since he was so furious at Jasper Dovel, very likely he should be an ally of Wade's. But Wade had no chance to explain that to him now.

The boy suddenly leaped past Wade and grabbed the pitchfork at the same time the old man did. 'You can't do that, Mr. Prandall!' he shouted. 'He'll shoot you.'

'I might as well be dead,' the old man said and tried to jerk the pitchfork away from the boy.

Wade lunged forward, using all his waning strength to reach the two before the old man got the pitchfork away from the boy. He got a hand on the fork and helped the boy jerk it away from the old man. The old man glared at Wade for a minute, then weaved over to a grain bin and sagged against it. He was a beaten man, hopelessness stamped clearly on his face.

As Wade got a better look at him, he realized he wasn't as old in years as he had thought, probably somewhere in his fifties. Then the name that the boy had called him struck home. Prandall. This must be the husband of Nancy Prandall and the father of Sue. No wonder he was almost out of his mind. But why take it out on Wade?

With a final glare at Wade, Prandall hunched himself away from the bin and stumbled out the door, turning up the street to the south.

'You'll have to allow for him, mister,' the boy said. 'His wife and daughter were killed in that stage wreck. How did you get out alive?'

'Pure luck,' Wade said. 'Nobody should have lived through that. Will you rent me a horse and tell me how to get to Dovel's?'

The boy nodded. 'Sure, mister. I ain't about to buck anything Mr. Dovel wants.'

'Prandall's liable to get himself killed the way he's acting.'

'I know. I don't think he cares. But you won't kill him, will you?'

'Don't figure on it,' Wade said. 'But I don't plan to let him run me through with a pitchfork, either.'

The boy brought out a saddled horse. 'You just ride up the street to the first corner then turn west. That street runs into a road that takes you straight to Dovel's ranch. It ain't far.'

Wade thanked him. 'How much rent for the horses?'

'Pay me when you get back,' the boy said, seeming anxious to get rid of him. 'Mr. Dovel will probably settle the bill.'

Wade swung into the saddle, feeling new pains from muscles that hadn't been taxed before. The horse was a good one, not too spirited. Wade guided him up the street, wondering if Prandall would find a gun and start shooting at him. His eyes swept the town. There was a church on his right before he reached the intersection. Across the street to the south of it was a bank, and diagonally across from the church was a hardware store. Wade's alertness doubled as he read the name across the false front, Prandall's Hardware.

He nudged the horse into a trot in spite of the jarring it gave him and turned the horse to the west. He half expected a shot from the hardware store, but Prandall evidently had gone inside and ignored the world around him. If he'd seen Wade riding up to the corner, he surely would have tried to kill him.

Once out of town, Wade relaxed a little until his thoughts turned to what lay ahead. Would Jasper Dovel know that Wade was an impostor? Even if he didn't, what would he expect of Wade? Had Hobie called the turn when he said that Dovel had hired Wade Vaun to kill Amos Burdeen?

Just a short distance from town, Wade saw a house and barn across the river to the north. From his cousin's description, he knew that must be the Runyan place where she and Brent had homesteaded. She had said it was just a half mile from town and across the creek. If so, that was the place Wade owned now. He was tempted to turn across the creek and look it over. But he was getting so tired and weak, he was beginning to doubt if he could stay in the saddle much longer as it was.

He rode another mile before he came to a big set of buildings. Some of them looked old enough to have been here for quite a while, but they were all in good repair. This would have to be Jasper Dovel's headquarters. The boy had said this road led right to it.

Wade was gripping the saddlehorn now to keep from falling off the horse. His head was swimming and he felt every bruise he had received in that fall. If Dovel's had been another half mile farther from town, he'd never have made it.

He started toward a big white house on a knoll when a man came out from a small house that stood fifty yards from the bigger one. He evidently was heading for the big barn with the acre of corrals on three sides of it when he saw Wade. He changed direction and came to meet him.

Wade reined up and started to dismount, but couldn't control his legs. The man jumped forward and caught him.

'You appear to be all in,' he said. 'Are you Wade Vaun?'

Wade nodded. 'I came to see Jasper Dovel.'

'I'll take you to him,' the man said. 'I'm Cal Fenton, his son-in-law. Can you walk by yourself?'

'I think so,' Wade said and pushed himself away from the horse.

A young woman came from the same house that Cal Fenton had just left and joined them. Cal Fenton was a small man and this woman was almost as big as he was. She had cold gray eyes that bored into Wade like bullets. This must be Fenton's wife. If so, she would be Jasper Dovel's daughter. Wade needed only one look to tell him she was the ruler of her roost.

'Who is he, Cal?' she demanded.

'Wade Vaun,' Fenton said. 'I'm taking him up to see your pa.'

'Vaun?' She looked him over from head to foot. 'He doesn't look like a killer to me.'

Wade met her glare. 'Lady, I don't get thrown over a bluff every day.'

She nodded. 'I reckon that could take some of the starch out of you. Come on. I'll take you up to see Pa. Maddie Fenton is my name. You've already met my husband.'

Wade nodded and followed Maddie toward the big house while Cal Fenton went on toward the barn. His knees were so weak he wondered if he would make it, but she didn't even look back. At the house, she walked in, leaving the door open for him to follow.

'He finally got here, Pa,' she called.

A big man in his sixties with gray hair and cold gray eyes exactly like those of his daughter loomed in the partition doorway. He sized up Wade like a hawk eyeing a squirrel.

'You look like you'd been pulled through a knothole backwards,' he said. 'But I reckon you'll come of it. How's your gun hand?'

'All right when I get strength enough to use it,' Wade said.

'I'm sure glad it was you that survived instead of that marshal,' Dovel said. 'Don't know why you both had to be on the same stage.'

'I didn't know he was going to be on it,' Wade said. 'I was lucky to live through it. The two Prandall women didn't.'

Jasper Dovel shrugged. 'Too bad about them. But it was worth it to get rid of that marshal. I wouldn't care if half the town had been killed, just so that tin star died.'

Wade had seldom heard more venom put into words. He knew what his fate would be if his real identity ever leaked out.

CHAPTER FIVE

Wade was led into a big room where a huge deer head above the fireplace held three rifles in its horns. He slumped into the chair indicated and tried to keep his wits about him. He was so weak and tired he wasn't sure he could think straight. But if he didn't, he could make a slip that would plant suspicion in Dovel's mind, and that would be the same as signing his own death warrant.

'You rode with that marshal for quite a ways, I reckon,' Dovel said when he had seated himself in his big chair and lit his pipe. 'Did he say anything about telling anyone he was coming here?'

Wade shook his head. 'He wasn't too talkative. Was he coming after you?'

'How do I know who he was after? I figure he was after whoever killed that dirt farmer across the creek from town. It wasn't long after Runyan's widow left here that we heard a marshal was coming to look into things. If there's anything we don't need here, it's a badge toter.'

'Don't you have any lawmen in Nevermore?'

'Sure,' Dovel said. 'Deuce Ulrich. But he sees what he's supposed to see and don't see nothing else. Hobie tells me you were holed up at Burdeen's place.'

Wade nodded. 'Burdeen's daughter found me down in the willows where I'd passed out. She and her father brought me to their place in a wagon. If they hadn't found me, I reckon I'd be dead now.'

Dovel grunted like a disappointed bear. 'I reckon I owe them a vote of thanks for that. But that's all they'll get. We don't need no squatters in this country. I've run this valley since I took it from the Indians and I don't figure on handing it over to no squatters now.'

'Did you hire me to run out people like that?'

'Not entirely,' Dovel said. 'I've got some other chores for you to do. Guess I didn't tell you much when I sent for you, so I'll lay it on the line now. When these squatters got so thick here, my sister, Kate Crudup, came to me with a proposition. She had lost her husband and she had two grown boys who were itching for a fight. They offered to move over here and help me keep control of the valley.'

'Are they getting too big for their britches?' Wade guessed.

Dovel bit down hard on his pipe stem. 'You might say that. They're good boys, not afraid of nothing, and they'll do any dirty job that comes along. But I'm not so sure they're going to be satisfied with the deal me and Kate made.'

Wade suddenly realized that Jasper Dovel had sent for Wade Vaun as a bodyguard for himself.

'They wouldn't bushwhack you, would they?'

'Naw, of course not,' Dovel said—but his voice sounded more like he was trying to convince himself than Wade. 'But they're ambitious and I can't stand anybody too ambitious. I'm in charge here, and it's going to stay that way. I figure they'll realize that when they see you riding with me.'

Wade wondered if Jasper Dovel was responsible for Brent Runyan's death. He insisted that he was in control of things here so, in a backhanded manner, he was accepting responsibility for everything that happened, including the death of Brent Runyan, whether he did the actual killing or not. He certainly was responsible for the departure or disappearance of several other homesteaders from the valley.

'Was it your orders that the stagecoach be forced off that bluff?'

Dovel puffed out several huge clouds of smoke from his pipe before he answered. 'I didn't know you were going to be on that stage,' he said finally.

'Why not?' Wade crowded him. 'You sent for me.'

He knew he had hit a nerve when he saw the frown on Dovel's face. Dovel hadn't ordered that wreck, but he wasn't going to admit that anybody had acted without his sanction. He'd obviously had other plans to get rid of the marshal, and he certainly hadn't wanted his own gunman killed. So it had been the Crudups who had planned that, hoping to get rid of both the marshal and Dovel's gunhand.

'How could I be sure which stage you'd be on?' Dovel grunted finally. 'Anyway, I'm glad they got the marshal.'

'Are you glad they killed that stage driver and the Prandall women, too?'

'What kind of question is that?' Dovel roared. 'They don't count. None of those sodbusters or two-bit storekeepers count. Were you sweet on that girl or something?'

'Hardly,' Wade said. 'But she did seem like a nice girl.'

Dovel took his pipe out of his mouth and used the stem to emphasize his words. 'Now you listen to me, Vaun. I hired you to work for me. You don't question what I order; you just do it. Is that clear?'

Wade stared at Dovel. 'I hear what you say,' he said. 'But I don't take too much talk like that from anybody.'

Dovel scowled and bristled like an angry dog, then slowly leaned back in his chair. 'I reckon I wouldn't have much use for a man who didn't have any spunk,' he grunted. 'We'll get along. You look tuckered. A day or two of rest will be the best thing for you now. Just keep ready in case you're needed.'

Wade nodded. Dovel roared for Sarah, and a woman about the size of Maddie Fenton came in. She was twenty-five years older than Maddie, but the resemblance was so close that Wade knew this had to be her mother. Sarah Dovel, however, didn't have the same hard, piercing eyes that her daughter possessed.

She motioned for Wade to follow her, and she led the way through two rooms to a bedroom in the back of the house. Wade hadn't realized till now how big this house was.

Mrs. Dovel pointed to a big ornamental iron bedstead. 'Better get in that bed and stay there. I'll bring your meals to you. You won't be any good to Jasper till you're able to ride all day and do whatever else he wants done.'

'Reckon that's right,' Wade said. 'That bed sure looks good.'

Wade stayed in the room for the next three days. The third day he was feeling pretty well, but he didn't tell Mrs. Dovel. Jasper didn't even come in to see how he was doing. He had no use for him till he was ready to work.

On the fourth day, Wade came out. He wasn't solving his own problem of identifying the man who had killed Brent Runyan.

There was no way of guessing what Jasper Dovel would demand of him once he reported ready for action. Wade hoped it would lead him to the evidence, that would convict the man who had killed Brent Runyan.

Before Jasper had a chance to give Wade any orders for the day, however, company arrived at the ranch. The two riders dismounted and tied their horses at the hitchrack.

'What do they want at this time of day?' Jasper Dovel grunted, slamming his chair back from the breakfast table and striding to the door.

Wade looked through the window at the visitors, but he didn't get up. He recognized Hobie Crudup, and the big heavy man with him must be his brother, Tank.

Jasper's greeting was cool when he invited his nephews into the house. But if there was any slight intended, the two younger men ignored it and tramped into the center of the room, glaring around until their attention centered on Wade.

'I see you got your gunnie,' Tank rumbled.

'Somebody had to do something,' Jasper

said. 'I've had some good reports on Wade Vaun.'

'We don't need no gun slick,' Hobie said. 'We can handle anything that comes up.'

'By killing everyone, I suppose?' Jasper said.

Tank scowled at Jasper. 'And just what do you expect your gunman to do, Uncle Jasper?'

'Scare the daylights out of people without having to draw his gun,' Jasper said quickly. 'Killing can get us in trouble, just like Runyan's killing brought in that marshal.'

Hobie grinned. 'Yeah, But you'll notice that the marshal didn't get here.'

'And Vaun just about didn't get here, either, thanks to you,' Jasper said angrily. 'Now you listen to me. I brought you two here to help me, not to try to run the show. I'm in charge and don't you forget it!'

Tank frowned at Jasper. 'I reckon we won't. We figure it's time to get the rest of the nesters out of the valley. Any objections?'

'Who have you got in mind?' Jasper asked, scowling.

'Ain't many left,' Tank said. 'Burdeen is the one closest to us and he's sitting there like a big fat toad and nobody's doing anything about it.'

'Hold on,' Jasper said, raising his hand. 'If it hadn't been for Burdeen nursing Vaun here, he might not have made it. I owe him something. Let him alone for a while.'

'For once, I agree with Uncle Jasper,' Hobie

said.

Tank wheeled on his brother. 'Just because you're sweet on that sodbuster's girl ain't no excuse for us getting soft. We're going to clear out everybody who's crowding us.'

Don't go off half cocked,' Dovel said, 'Another killing will bring in a swarm of marshals. No telling what will happen because of that stage wreck. Once word gets back that a marshal died in that wreck, you can bet some badge toter will come to see about it.'

'Nobody lived through it but your gunnie. If he keeps his mouth shut, what can anybody prove?' Hobie glared at Wade. 'How about it, Vaun?'

'I'm not blabbing about it,' Wade said.

'The Burdeens know,' Tank reminded them. 'Let's get rid of them.'

'I'll see to it they don't talk,' Hobie said.

'Since that Burdeen girl took such good care of Uncle Jasper's gun slick, maybe she took a shine to him,' Tank said. 'Where would that leave you, Hobie?'

Hobie scowled. 'If she did, I'll kill them all myself.'

'Let's find out what she thinks,' Tank challenged.

'Shut up!' Jasper shouted. 'You'll do what I say. And I say let them alone right now.'

'Maybe you figure on having your gunhand take care of things,' Hobie said.

'If necessary,' Jasper said. 'Or don't you

think he can do it?'

Tank shrugged. 'Anybody can kill a sodbuster. It's no skin off our noses if you want to pay a gunman for doing something we would do for nothing.'

Wade could easily see how he rated with the Crudups. The fact that he was with Jasper Dovel wasn't going to lessen their efforts to kill him.

'We'll check with the Burdeens to find out how much your gunnie told them,' Tank said.

'Let Hobie do that checking,' Jasper said.

'I agree with that, Uncle Jasper,' Hobie said. 'Tank would just foul things up.'

The two went outside. Jasper turned to Wade. 'Do you feel up to riding now?'

Wade nodded. 'Sure. I'm still sore in a few places, but that's all.'

'I want you to ride into town and nose around. The townspeople brought in the bodies from that wreck. Find out if there's any talk about a marshal being killed. If news of that gets back where he came from, there will be more marshals swarming around Nevermore. We don't want that.'

'We sure don't,' Wade agreed.

He went outside. On this first assigment, he agreed wholeheartedly with Jasper Dovel. He certainly didn't want any marshal coming to investigate the death of Marshal Wade Tillotson. It wouldn't take long till the news would get out that the dead man was not Wade

Tillotson. Wade wouldn't give a plugged nickel for his chances if Jasper Dovel and the Crudups found out they were harboring a marshal instead of a hired killer.

Wade saddled the horse that the ranch flunkey caught for him and headed for town. From the looks of the bunkhouse out by the cookshack, Wade guessed that the ranch had a large number of riders.

The horse wasn't the fastest one Wade had ever ridden, but he was gentle and an easy rider. Wade was thankful for both. He still didn't feel up to a battle with a salty bronc.

It took only a short time to cover the mile and a half to Nevermore. Before reaching town, he had decided that the town marshal was the one to see to find out if word had been sent out that Marshal Tillotson had been killed in the stage wreck.

Reaching the intersection of Main Street, Wade reined his horse to the right away from the river. Most of the businesses of town were along this block. Only the livery barn and the church were north toward the river.

His eyes turned toward Prandall's Hardware, the first store on his left as he turned south. The door was closed and the place had every appearance of being locked up. The bank on his right was open but he ignored it.

His eyes raced up and down the street. There was no telling what reaction the people of the town would have to Jasper Dovel's hired gun. And there was the possibility that the Crudups might be in town. Although they hadn't threatened him at Dovel's this morning, there was no doubt in Wade's mind what they would do if they caught him away from Dovel. They had said they were going to go down to Burdeens', at least, Hobie was, and the town of Nevermore was between Dovel's ranch and Burdeens'.

The building south of Prandall's on the east was vacant, and so was the building south of the bank on the west side of the street. That bore out what Wade had heard about Nevermore fading away. A barber shop sat on the west side of the street, south of the vacant building. Across the street from it was a fairly large building with 'Skarsten Grocery' painted across its false front. That must be the store owned by Herman Skarsten, the stage driver.

On the corner lots were the hotel and stage station on the west side and the marshal's office and the town jail on the east. Wade headed for the marshal's office.

Swinging down, he crossed the little porch to the door which was open. Inside he found a man of average height but much overweight slumped in his chair behind a big desk, sound asleep. As Wade stamped across the floor to the desk, the man jerked awake with a snort and glared up at his visitor.

'Are you Marshal Deuce Ulrich?' Wade

asked.

The man scowled. 'Why else do you think I'd be here?' He rubbed a sleeve across the star sagging on his shirt front. 'What do you want?'

Wade was sure, now that he got a look at the marshal, that he was one of the men who had come out to take the bodies in from the stage wreck the other day. Wade had carefully kept out of sight that afternoon.

'I just came from Jasper Dovel's ranch,' Wade said and saw the marshal straighten noticeably. 'He wants to know what the town is saying about the stage wreck.'

'Just talking, that's all,' Deuce said. 'You know how that goes, especially when some well-known people are killed. There was a big crowd at the church for Nancy and Sue Prandall's funeral, and almost as many the next morning for Herman Skarsten's funeral.'

'What about the marshal that was killed?'

'Well, we planted him a couple of hours after we buried Herman. No funeral, just the preacher saying a few words at the grave.'

'What about notifying the marshal's office back in Wheeler that he had been killed?'

'If you work for Mr. Dovel, you know I wouldn't do that without asking him and he told me not to tell anyone. But I did have my daughter, Fanny, make a drawing of the man's face just in case Mr. Dovel wanted him identified sometime.'

'That's not likely,' Wade said. 'Just how good is your daughter at drawing?'

Pride erased the worried frown on the marshal's face. 'Pretty good. She's got the picture over at the house or I'd show you. She can draw anybody as good as one of those picture takers can do with a camera.'

Wade guessed that was mostly parental pride talking, but it was possible that she was good enough to draw a recognizable likeness of a man. Wade had a hunch that Deuce Ulrich had the heart of a blackmailer, and he had an idea that he might be able to use that picture someday to put some feathers in his own nest.

Although he seemed completely loyal to Jasper Dovel, it must be Dovel he had in mind to blackmail. It had surely been Dovel he had run to with the news that a marshal was coming after Wade had contacted him. Wade doubted if he knew that it had been the Crudups and not Jasper Dovel who had wrecked that stage. Dovel was too proud to admit that they had acted without his orders. He wouldn't allow anyone to know that he was not absolute master of all he surveyed, including his nephews.

'If I were you, I'd be mighty careful who I showed that picture to,' Wade said. 'Were you contacted by this marshal before he came?'

Deuce nodded and Wade knew then that he wasn't going to lie. 'I sure was. That was his first mistake. His second mistake was coming here. He didn't live to make a third one.'

'You make mighty sure that word of his death doesn't get out of town,' Wade warned.

'I'll do my best,' Deuce said. 'You tell Mr. Dovel that.'

Wade went back inside. He wondered how long it would take for Ike Yancey or some other lawman to hear about the wreck. If another lawman, especially Yancy, showed up, Wade's secret would be out. He had to find out who killed Brent Runyan and arrest him before that happened. Once Dovel and the Crudups found out who he really was, they'd be after him like starving birds after a grasshopper.

Wade stepped into Skarsten's Grocery, next to the marshal's office. He hoped to find out what the people of town were thinking about the wreck. Deuce hadn't been much help in telling him how the people felt or how much they knew.

Whatever he expected, he certainly wasn't prepared for what he ran into. The light was poor inside the store, but he had no trouble identifying the shotgun that was pointed at him over the counter.

'Get out of here!' the woman shouted. 'I don't want anybody connected with Jasper Dovel inside my store.'

Wade stopped dead in his tracks. The woman was fairly tall and about forty with auburn hair and blue eyes. She was not a bad-looking woman, but right now she looked like the angel of death to Wade.

'Don't do it, Effie,' another woman said and Wade turned his eyes enough to see Cozetta down the counter from Effie Skarsten.

The gun didn't waver and Wade didn't move as Cozetta came down the counter and gently pushed the barrel of the gun aside.

'He may be Jasper Dovel's hired killer, but he didn't cause the wreck that killed Herman,' Cozetta said gently. 'He was in the wreck, too. Almost got killed.'

'I wish he had,' Effie said. 'If it wasn't for Dovel and his bullheaded determination to hog the whole range, there wouldn't have been any stage wreck because there wouldn't have been any need of a U. S. marshal coming to Nevermore.'

'I know, Effie,' Cozetta said. 'But don't get yourself hanged for killing somebody as unimportant as a hired gunman.'

'Maybe you're right,' Effie said. 'He ain't worth that. If I'm going to kill somebody, I'll kill old Jasper himself.'

Cozetta looked at Wade. 'You'd better get out. If there's anything you want to buy, come back later.'

'Not sure that I want anything here bad enough to face that gun again,' Wade said. 'What are you doing here?'

'I work here,' Cozetta said. She looked at Effie as she put the gun down and went back to the rear room of the store. 'I've helped Effie for a year while Herman was driving the stage. She's terribly upset now. If I were you, I wouldn't cross her again.'

'You can bet I won't,' Wade said.

He stepped through the door onto the porch. As he started up the street, he saw Tank Crudup riding toward him from the livery barn. Tank had seen him and Wade knew he was in for some real trouble.

CHAPTER SIX

Wade had wanted to check Prandall's store to see if Prandall was there. But he forgot that when he saw Tank Crudup spur his horse forward. Wade wondered if Tank would try to kill him right here on the street, or wait until he could do it where no one would see so Jasper Dovel couldn't prove that Tank had done it. Maybe Tank and Hobie felt that they could control Jasper if they could get rid of his hired gun. Jasper must share that feeling or he wouldn't have sent for Wade Vaun in the first place.

The building next to Skarsten's was empty and Wade dodged down the alley between it and Skarsten's. Before Tank could get up even with the narrow alley, Wade had gone behind the building. He tried the back door and found it unlocked. He stepped inside and shut the door.

Waiting there, he listened. He heard the horse stop out in the street and a man moved down the alley on foot, obviously trying to be quiet, but the noises he made were as easy for Wade to follow as the progress of an elephant. The man hesitated at the back of the building.

Wade had his gun in his hand. If this was a showdown, Wade welcomed it. Tank was one of the men who had crowded the stage off the bluff, so Wade had a score to settle with him.

He thought of trying to arrest Tank for wrecking the stage and killing four people. But there had been three men involved in that. He'd better get Hobie Crudup and Luke Edris at the same time if he was going to make an arrest. He really wasn't ready to make an arrest yet, anyway. The moment he did that, he'd reveal his identity and his chances of finding the man who killed Brent Runyan would be gone.

Wade waited, gun ready, as Tank apparently had trouble making a decision whether to barge into the building or not. He must know that Wade was inside. He'd also realize his disadvantage because Wade would be waiting for him. Wade Vaun had the reputation of a killer or Jasper Dovel wouldn't have hired him.

Footsteps finally retraced themselves down the alley. Tank apparently had decided there would be a better and safer time to face

Jasper's hired gun.

Wade waited until he heard the horse walk away from the front of the building, then he went back through the door and moved out to the street. Tank was nowhere in sight. Still Wade moved carefully. Tank could be waiting somewhere to ambush him.

As Wade reached his horse in front of the marshal's office, Cozetta came out of the grocery store next door.

'Was Tank trying to find you,?' she asked.

'Reckon he was,' Wade said. 'But I don't want to start a civil war among Dovel's outfit.'

'Wish somebody would,' Cozetta said. 'Hobie says that Tank is pretty mad at Mr. Dovel for hiring a fast gun.'

'Hobie's not too happy about it, either,' Wade agreed. 'Have you seen George Prandall?'

Cozetta shook her head. 'Not lately. He hasn't opened his store since the funeral. I've seen him once and he looks terrible, like a madman.'

Wade nodded. 'If you see Tank, tell him I'll be out at Dovel's if he wants to find me.'

He mounted and rode south out of town. If Tank was planning to ambush him, he'd likely do it along the regular road, maybe at the edge of town. By going south, Wade wouldn't be riding near the established road to the ranch.

Wade decided against telling Dovel about Tank's appearance in town. He had no proof that Tank was out to kill him, even though he was sure of it. He only reported that Deuce had told no one of the marshal's death and it wasn't likely that word would work its way back to headquarters for quite a while, at least.

Shortly after dinner, a rider charged up to the hitchrack in front of the house and Jasper looked out the window and swore. Wade glanced through the window at the woman swinging down from the horse. She was dressed in Levi's, an old shirt and a flop-brimmed hat.

'Who's that?' Wade asked.

'My sister, Kate,' Dovel said with no sign of happiness.

Wade took another look. So that was Kate Crudup. He'd heard quite a bit about her; now he was going to meet her.

She stamped up the steps and banged the door open as if was her own home. She stared around the room, shifted the gun on her hip like a man, then strode in, flopping in a chair across the room from Jasper.

'Boys come by this morning?' she asked.

'They did,' Jasper said. 'Tank was all set to wipe out the Burdeen family.'

'What's wrong with that?' Kate demanded.

Jasper scowled. 'In the first place, they took care of the new man I hired, Wade Vaun here. In the second place, we don't want a whole swarm of marshals riding in here. Another murder like Brent Runyan's and the country will be crawling with lawmen.'

'Don't blame me or the boys for killing Runyan,' Kate said. 'You were the one who wanted him dead. By the way, I'm letting Tank and Tunie move into the Runyan place.'

Jasper leaned forward in his chair. 'Why? Don't you and Tunie get along? Do you want her out of your house?'

'Naw,' Kate said with a shrug. 'Tunie ain't worth a pinch of salt, but Tank married her so he's stuck with her. But five of us, counting Luke, are just too many for that little house you put us in.'

'It was the best house in the valley that was empty,' Jasper said.

'Maybe so. But there's a better house now—Runyan's. I'm settled where I am and Hobie and Luke ain't home enough to care what the place is like. So Tank and Tunie are the ones to move into Runyan's.'

Jasper stared shrewdly at his sister. 'Are you trying to flank me on both sides? You live to the west; Runyan's place is to the east.'

'I ain't flanking nobody,' Kate said as if the accusation didn't bother her at all. 'But somebody has to keep an eye on that town. You know how many people in Nevermore would love to see you dead. Me and the boys, too, for that matter. Runyan's place is within half a mile of town. Tank and Tunie can see what's going on there if they live that close.'

'You sicked those boys onto that stage,

didn't you?' Jasper accused after a minute's pause.

'So what?' Kate said with another shrug. 'You wanted that marshal dead, didn't you? I heard you say so. With everybody on it killed, there wasn't going to be any witnesses as to what happened. All that came out alive is that killer you hired there.'

'You blamed near killed him, too.' Jasper said angrily. 'But he ain't talking. He just came from town where he checked with Deuce. Deuce ain't going to send out word that the marshal is dead.'

'Word will get out eventually,' Kate said. 'If nothing else, when that marshal doesn't report back, they're going to come looking for him. We'd better have things well covered up by then. That's why we've got to get rid of the Burdeen family. They know all about that wreck—they nursed your man there. He very likely told them exactly what happened.'

'All right, all right,' Jasper said, waving a hand. 'But some people in town may know now, too. That girl, Cozetta, works in Effie's store.'

'Now you're wising up,' Kate said. 'We've got to get rid of people like the Burdeens who know too much. And we'll either scare the rest of the people till they are afraid to talk, or fix them so they can't talk. It's that simple.'

'You're bloodthirsty,' Jasper said and Wade wasn't sure whether the words were prompted by shock or admiration.

'I'm your sister. What can you expect?'

Jasper suddenly changed the course of the conversation. 'I've heard stories of Brent Runyan's ghost running loose over at his place. What will Tunie think of that?'

Kate's face sobered and turned a little gray. 'Who says so?' she demanded.

'I heard it the last time I was in town,' Jasper said, satisfaction in his voice. 'Tunie won't live where there are ghosts, will she?'

'I doubt it,' Kate said. 'And I can't say that I blame her. Ghosts are bad medicine.' She stared at Jasper. 'You're just making that up to keep Tank and Tunie from moving there.'

Jasper shook his head. 'No, I'm not. Just let them move there and see.'

'They will be moving there in another day or two. I ain't going to tell them that crazy story about Runyan's ghost, either.'

Kate got up and headed for the door, obviously shaken by Jasper's report of a ghost in the Runyan place. If she'd had other business with her brother, apparently it was forgotten when she heard his ghost story.

Wade watched her ride away then turned to Jasper. 'What's this about a ghost at Runyan's?'

Jasper grinned. 'Don't tell me you're afraid of ghosts, too?'

'Never thought about it,' Wade said. 'What have you got for me to do now?'

Jasper rubbed his chin. 'Nothing, I guess. If you want to look around a bit, go ahead. Just be back by the middle of the afternoon. I figure Tank and Hobie might be along about then. I want you to get acquainted with them.'

Wade nodded. He knew how Jasper wanted him to get acquainted with his nephews. More and more, he realized that Jasper Dovel had sent for Wade Vaun simply as a safeguard against his own nephews.

Wade got his horse and rode toward town. A short distance from the ranch, he swung his horse off the road and across the creek, riding east along the north bank. He wanted to take a good look at Brent Runyan's place before Tank Crudup and his wife moved in. His cousin had left in a hurry, and she had told him of some of the valuable things that she had left behind. In fact, she had rushed to town the day Brent had been killed and not gone back for anything, even selling what livestock she owned to a man right there in town. She was sure that anything that was missing from the house would probably be in the possession of the man who killed Brent.

Wade wasn't too sure of that, but possession of Brent's things would direct suspicion toward that man, all right. If he wasn't the killer, he at least was a thief.

It hadn't been so long since Brent was killed. Perhaps there might still be some clue around the place that would lead Wade to the killer. It was worth checking out, Wade decided.

The place still looked neat and well-kept except for weeds starting to grow near the house and barn now. The house was in good shape. Wade found the door unlocked and went inside. Brent Runyan was one of the few homesteaders in the country who had been able to afford a frame house. His barn and hog shed were of sod, but they were empty now.

Inside the house, Wade made a quick survey. Some of the things that his cousin had told him about were in sight. But one thing she especially valued, Brent's pearl-handled revolver, was missing.

Wade made a thorough search of the house but didn't find the gun. He had the feeling that the killer likely had gone through the house after Brent's wife left and, if he saw that gun, he'd have taken it. Possession of the pearl-handled gun would not be proof that the man was the killer, but it would give Wade a place to start his investigation. He'd watch for that gun.

Going back outside, Wade squinted at the sun. He had plenty of time. He wondered about the tunnel his cousin had told him about, She said that Brent had dug it when it became apparent that Jasper Dovel was determined to drive them out of the country. There was a trap door in the kitchen of the house, she said, that led into the tunnel. The tunnel ran down to the creek, its mouth in the bank there.

Wade walked down to the creek and jumped off the bank, which was about four feet high at that point and had water willows growing close to it in places. Moving along the bank, he finally found the tunnel opening. He would never have seen it if he hadn't been searching for it. Brent had piled several cottonwood branches in front of the opening so that it looked like a place where someone had dumped a load of tree limbs. Water willows were growing near the mouth of the tunnel. No casual passerby was liable to see that tunnel opening.

Wade pushed aside some of the branches and looked inside. The interior of the tunnel was pitch black, but it seemed dry. Brent Runyan had put a lot of work on that tunnel, but he hadn't gotten the chance to use it.

Wade rode back to Dovel's ranch, only a mile up the creek on the other side. Tying his horse in front of the house, he loosened the cinch and went inside. He expected to find Jasper Dovel there, but the house appeared to be empty. Wade lost no time wondering where everyone was. He began a careful look around. That pearl-handled revolver might be here, if Jasper Dovel or one of his trusted men had killed Brent Runyan.

Wade might have been caught prowling

around if Dovel hadn't stormed into the house like an angry bull. Wade quickly slipped out of the inner office where he had been looking for the revolver. He was in the living room when Dovel arrived, his face dark and flushed.

'We've got some sneaking cattle thieves in this valley,' he roared at Wade. 'Andy just told me fifty head are missing from my west pasture.'

'That sounds like too many for homesteaders to be taking,' Wade said.

'Maybe. Maybe not.' Dovel dropped heavily into his chair. 'They were there this morning, Andy said. So this time we're going to find out who took them. Andy is rounding up some men to go after them. You'll go along.'

'Have you lost cattle before?' Wade asked.

'Andy says he's sure of it. Can't really tell till we have a round-up.'

'Are there enough homesteaders still here to be doing that?'

'It doesn't take many men to run off a herd of cattle,' Dovel grunted. 'Of course, it could be somebody else who wants to see me broke.'

'Who would that be?' Wade pressed.

Dovel was on the point of answering but then he scowled at Wade and shook his head. 'No telling. A man stirs up a lot of enemies when he works as hard as I have to build this spread.'

A rider charged into the yard and Wade stepped to the window, expecting to see

Dovel's foreman, Andy Kent. But it was the town marshal, Deuce Ulrich.

'Wonder what Deuce wants,' he said.

Dovel's head snapped up. 'It won't make any difference what he wants,' he said. 'He's going after my cattle. That will put the law on our side when we hang those thieves.'

Wade almost said that the law didn't hang men until convicted, but he checked himself. Wade Vaun was supposed to be as lawless as any man Jasper Dovel had on his payroll.

Deuce Ulrich banged into the house without knocking and hurried to the living room where Dovel spent much of his time. 'George Prandall hasn't showed up out here, has he?' Deuce demanded.

'No,' Dovel said. 'Why should he?'

'He's gone crazy as a hoot owl,' Deuce said. 'Swears he's going to kill every man who is responsible for the deaths of his wife and daughter. He's aiming to start with you and the Crudup boys.' He looked at Wade. 'And I reckon he might kill you, too, if you get in his way.'

Wade nodded. He was sure he was on Prandall's list. Wade worked for Jasper Dovel and that burned him with the same killer brand that marked Dovel and the Crudups in the eyes of the people of Nevermore, especially George Prandall.

'He hasn't been out here,' Dovel said then dismissed the subject. 'Somebody ran off fifty of my best steers today, Deuce. You're going with my men to get them back. And if you don't hang the thieves, I'll find me another marshal for Nevermore.'

'But I've got to get back to town,' Deuce sputtered. 'Got to keep an eye out for Prandall.'

'You've got to get my cattle back and hang those thieves!' Dovel thundered. 'Do you understand?'

The marshal nodded hastily. A rumble of hooves in the yard marked the arrival of Andy Kent with several men of Dovel's crew. Without another word, Deuce spun on his heel and headed for the door. Wade followed him.

Wade tightened the cinch on his saddle and swung up. He looked back at the house. Jasper Dovel was on the porch, glaring at the men. Wade had the feeling he was staring directly at him.

As he rode out of the yard with Dovel's men, he wondered if perhaps Jasper Dovel had discovered that Wade was an impostor and had sent him along on this mission with instructions to his foreman to see to it that he didn't come back. Wade knew he could be riding into a trap. But he saw no way to avoid it if that was the way it was.

CHAPTER SEVEN

Andy Kent led out, with the men strung along behind him. There were still a few hours of daylight. With good luck, they might overtake the rustlers before dark. If not, maybe they could get a line on the direction the cattle were being taken and ride on into the night.

There seemed to be nothing on Kent's mind but finding the rustlers' trail and keeping on it. Wade chided himself for being too skittish. But he knew he couldn't afford even one mistake. If Jasper Dovel got suspicious of him, he'd begin putting things together and come up with a conclusion that would mean a bullet for Wade.

They struck the trail where it left the west pasture and Kent followed it at an easy gallop. There weren't many places on this prairie where the rustlers could hide a herd of fifty cattle. Wade didn't doubt that they'd find the herd. He was more than passingly curious as to who they would find with the herd. He doubted if there were enough homesteaders around to attempt a rustling job like this. Even if there were, they'd be afraid to leave their homesteads unguarded this long.

Jasper obviously didn't trust his sister's sons. Wade was sure that Jasper had come close to admitting as much to him an hour ago when he'd almost given him the names of someone other than the homesteaders who might be stealing his cattle. After seeing Kate Crudup, Wade wouldn't put it past her to be stealing cattle from her brother.

There had been some effort made to hide the trail of the cattle by driving them along the rocky ledges near the creek, and usually the trail led along the low places, the creek bed and gullies. But Kent had no difficulty following as long as it was light.

The sun went down and still the cattle were not in sight. Whoever had taken them knew how to get them over the ground fast. They were more than fifteen miles from Dovel's ranch now.

Then just before darkness, the trail disappeared on a rocky ledge near the creek. Kent called a halt and rode out in a big circle.

'They turned north here,' he said, coming back. 'Reckon they figured anybody following them wouldn't get here till after dark. We made it just in time. They're heading for the railroad at Madison, I'd guess.'

They swung north as darkness closed down and within an hour heard cattle bawling ahead. They proceeded slower then, and more cautiously. Wade guessed it was sometime after nine o'clock when they finally caught up with the herd. The rustlers were still pushing the cattle along, although they were making poor progress now. The cattle were tired and kept trying to turn aside and stop.

The moon was almost full and Wade could see the herd fairly well. He could locate only three men with the herd. Under good conditions, three men could handly fifty head without much difficulty. But these drivers were having their troubles now with the weary cattle.

'Let's hit them,' Kent shouted and dug in his spurs.

The cattle heard the commotion almost as soon as the rustlers did. They scattered and the three drivers dug in their spurs and shot straight ahead, forgetting the cattle. Guns roared and, if the cattle hadn't been so tired, there would have been a stampede. But they merely got out of the way of the onrushing riders and let them pass.

The men ahead seemed to have good horses, or else the sudden excitement gave them fresh energy. Within two minutes they were out of sight, disappearing into some gullies. After ten minutes of futile searching, Kent called a halt.

'Let's take the cattle back,' he said. 'Anybody recognize any of them?'

Nobody said anything. Finally, Deuce volunteered an opinion. 'One of them was mighty big,' he said.

'A lot of men are big,' another man said. 'I thought that one fellow I got closest to might have been Luke Edris. Luke is left handed and this fellow had his gun in his left hand.'

Wade had decided that the big one could

easily have been Tank Crudup. He didn't know about Luke Edris being left handed, but if that was so, that would account for two of the rustlers. Wade didn't think the other man had looked like Hobie. More than likely Hobie had stayed around Nevermore and let himself be seen to establish an alibi for the Crudups.

Even Tank had been in Nevermore this morning. Wade had seen him there. But he would have had time since then to have caught up with the rustlers if the whole thing had been planned beforehand, and Wade was willing to bet it had been. Hobie and Tank had been at Jasper Dovel's early this morning and had established the fact that they were going on to Burdeen's from there.

They got the cattle home sometime near morning. Wade was dog tired, as were the other riders. Deuce Ulrich stayed at Dovel's for the rest of the night rather than ride the last mile and a half to town.

It was ten o'clock before Wade awoke. He lay still for a minute trying to decide what had wakened him. It was strange to find himself in bed at this hour, but it was not that strangeness that had roused him. Then he heard someone coming up the gravel walk to the door. He climbed out of bed and dressed quickly, then hurried out into the living room to find Jasper Dovel facing a young woman Wade had never seen before.

'This is Fanny Ulrich,' Dovel said when

Wade appeared. 'She came out to find her father. Fanny, this is my new hired hand, Wade Vaun.'

'I've heard about him,' Fanny said.

She was a slim girl with red hair and blue eyes. Only her nose and the general contour of her face held any resemblance to her father. Her mother must have been a beauty, Wade decided. She certainly, didn't get her good looks from Deuce.

'Why don't you two go for a ride or something while we wait for Deuce to wake up?' Jasper, suggested.

Fanny laughed. 'I see you know how grumpy Pa can be when somebody wakes him before he's ready. I'm willing if Mr. Vaun is.'

Wade shrugged. Jasper obviously was uncomfortable with Fanny Ulrich in the house. Wade would have preferred to have some breakfast first, but he wanted to know more about Fanny Ulrich. Deuce had said she was good at drawing and had made a sketch of the dead man killed in the stage wreck. He'd like to see that and make sure it wasn't sent to anyone who would recognize that it wasn't Wade Tillotson.

Wade went out to the corral and caught and saddled a horse. Fanny met him there with her horse.

'Where shall we ride?' she asked.

'Doesn't make any difference to me,' Wade said. 'It seems that the important thing to

Jasper was that we get out of the house.'

'I had that feeling, too,' Fanny said, laughing. 'But then I don't enjoy staying in there, either. Don't see how his wife stands it all day.'

They rode up the river. Wade enjoyed Fanny's company. She seemed entirely uninhibited and talked almost constantly. When she slowed down as if running out of small talk, Wade asked about her hobby of drawing.

'If you'll pose for me, I'll show you,' she said.

They dismounted and Wade stood beside his horse while Fanny took a pad and pencil out of her saddle bag. Within five minutes she handed him the pad. He was astonished at the likeness of himself. He knew now that Deuce hadn't exaggerated his daughter's talents. If she had drawn Wade Vaun's picture as well as this, anyone seeing it would recognize Vaun if they knew him. Or if they knew Wade Tillotson, they'd know that the picture wasn't of him.

'Let's get back and see if dinner is ready,' Fanny said. 'If we go any farther up the creek, we'll be near Crudups'. And I don't want to run into Tank or Kate.'

'I couldn't agree with you more,' Wade said.

Deuce was up when they got back, but Wade had the feeling that Jasper had gotten him up. He was sour-faced and grumpy. Sarah Dovel had dinner on the table and Wade ate like a hungry wolf. He hadn't had anything to eat since yesterday noon.

'See you around?' Fanny said when she mounted to ride back to town with her father. It was more of a question than statement.

'I'll be in town and I'll look you up.'

'We live just a block east of Pa's office,' Fanny said.

'She don't need no company when I'm not there,' Deuce said sourly.

'I come over to Pa's office quite often,' Fanny said quickly.

Wade understood. She'd come to the marshal's office if he happened to stop there. He'd stop, all right. Fanny had a loose tongue and she knew a lot about what was going on. He might find out more from her than he could from his own investigating.

'I'd like to know if Tank and Tunie are moving into the Runyan place,' Jasper said later that afternoon. 'Ride down that way and see.'

Wade nodded. He'd been thinking about riding into town to see that picture of Vaun that Fanny had drawn. This gave him the excuse he was looking for to get away from the ranch.

Getting his horse, he rode down the valley toward Nevermore. As he came opposite the Runyan place he saw a wagon backed up to the front door of the house. Evidently Tank and his wife were moving in. Once Wade established his true identity, he'd have the pleasure of throwing Tank Crudup out of that place, if he hadn't already arrested him.

Riding on into town, Wade turned into Main Street, glancing again at the closed doors of Prandall's hardware store. He wondered where George Prandall was. He hadn't heard any more about him since Deuce had said he was out to get revenge. Riding on past Skarsten's Grocery, he reined in at the marshal's office. Before he had tied his horse, he saw Fanny coming from a house a block east of Main Street. He waited for her on the walk.

'Saw you riding in,' Fanny said when she reached him. 'Got business with Pa? Or can we visit a while?'

'Matter of fact, I really came to see you,' Wade said.

'There's a nice bench right here in the shade,' Fanny said. 'Let's sit and gab.'

Wade looked down the street. 'Won't this set tongues wagging—you spending your time visiting with Dovel's hired killer?'

'Let them wag,' Fanny said. 'They've got to be talking about somebody.'

'I get the idea from what Jasper says that he runs this valley with a iron hand. Is that the way you see it?'

'It's been that way ever since we came here. But now the Crudup boys figure in it, too. They get mighty high-handed once in a while and they don't always toe the line that Jasper draws.' She giggled. 'Makes it sort of interesting trying to guess what might happen one of these days.'

'Do you think Jasper killed Brent Runyan? Or did the Crudups?'

She turned and looked squarely at him. 'That's a funny question for you to be asking. You take your orders from Jasper. What does he say?'

'Nothing. That's why I'm asking. I'm a curious cuss, as you can see.'

'Nothing wrong with that. I'm curious, too. Jasper hires people to do his killing. You ought to know that. I figure the Crudup boys did this one—with Jasper's approval. I doubt if they had his approval for wrecking the stage.'

'From what he said to his sister, I know they didn't,' Wade agreed.

He changed the subject. 'I'd like to see that drawing your pa said you made of the dead marshal.'

'It's over at the house,' Fanny said. 'Pa wouldn't like it if I took you over there when he wasn't there. Ma's dead, you know. How about you coming to our place for supper tomorrow night? I can cook, too.'

'I'd like that,' Wade said. 'Of course, if Jasper keeps me at the ranch, I can't do much about that.'

'If he does, I'll skin him myself,' Fanny said. 'I'll be looking for you.'

The door of Skarsten's Grocery swung open and Cozetta came out, looking over at Wade and Fanny.

'Hello, Cozetta,' Fanny said as she got up. 'I'm just going home. You want to talk to Wade for a while?'

Cozetta stared at Fanny. 'No,' she said frigidly. 'I have nothing to say to him.' She wheeled back into the store. Fanny laughed and winked at Wade before disappearing down the little alley between the marshal's office and the store.

Wade went back to his horse. For some reason, Cozetta had been as mad as a wet hen. He didn't see what difference it made to Cozetta who he talked to. She had certainly let him know what she thought of him, a hired killer for Jasper Dovel.

He mounted and rode slowly out of town. He had learned a little more from Fanny. He had the feeling she had a pretty good idea what was going on. She didn't think it was Jasper Dovel who had killed Brent Runyan, but she thought he had given his approval. If he hadn't done it, then it must have been one of the Crudups. If one of them was guilty, then he had to find out which one.

When he rode into the yard at Dovel's, he was met by Jasper, beside himself with fury.

'What took you so long?' he roared. 'Do you know that crazy Prandall tried to kill me while you were gone? Almost did it, too. Sneaked up to the house and shot at me through the window. Hit my chair and didn't miss my head more than an inch.'

'I probably wouldn't have seen him if I'd been here,' Wade said.

'Maybe not,' Dovel said. 'But if you'd been here, you could have caught him. We'd have hung him higher than a kite.'

'You sent me down to see if Tank was moving into the Runyan place,' Wade reminded him. 'He is. I saw his wagon up by the house.'

'I could have walked down there and back in the time you've been gone. Now I want you to get out and find Prandall. Get him before he kills all of us!'

Wade reined his horse around and headed down the creek. He doubted very much if Prandall would go back to Nevermore. He'd know Dovel's men would look for him there. Wade wasn't particularly anxious to find him, anyway. He sympathized with him. Wade could imagine how he would feel if he had lost a wife and daughter in a wreck deliberately caused like that stage wreck had been. Maybe Jasper Dovel wasn't to blame for that wreck, but he was to blame for bringing in the Crudups who did do it. Prandall had good reason for striking at Jasper Dovel.

Wade got back to the ranch late that night. He reported his failure to find Prandall and Jasper swore lustily.

'You're not trying very hard,' he said finally, curbing his anger. 'There just aren't that many places around here where a man can hide.'

'I don't know this country like you do,' Wade said. 'Somebody who knows the country could hide from me easily enough.'

Jasper grunted his reluctant agreement with that and headed off to bed.

Wade was up at his usual hour the next morning. He supposed Dovel would either send him out again this morning to look for Prandall, or keep him right here at the ranch to stand guard over him.

He found that Dovel had decided on the latter course. Wade whiled away the morning moving around the ranch yard from building to building, watching for anyone trying to sneak up to the house. Since Prandall had come so close to success once, Dovel was sure he would try again. Prandall was crazy, everyone said, so he wouldn't reason like a logical man.

No one showed up and at mid-afternoon, Dovel sent Wade to town to get supplies for the ranch. He gave Wade orders to search the town thoroughly for Prandall while he was there.

Wade rode into town, on the alert. Jasper Dovel wasn't the only man on George Prandall's list. He had made one attempt to kill Wade. He'd probably make another if Wade got careless.

The town was quiet as Wade rode in. He

reined up in front of Effie Skarsten's store. He wondered if she would run him out again as she had done before. If so, where was Dovel going to get supplies for his ranch? The answer was obvious. He'd send Andy Kent and his men in and they'd just take what they needed. Wade doubted if they'd even pay for what they took.

Dismounting, Wade went into the store. Just inside the door he stopped, his hand dropping to his gun.

Back near the rear of the store he saw Cozetta talking to Hobie Crudup. Wade didn't seen any extra horses in town, so he hadn't expected to find any of the Crudups here.

He saw Cozetta lay a hand on Hobie's arm, and Hobie relaxed as he looked at Wade. Wade relaxed a bit, too, and moved up to the counter. Cozetta apparently could control Hobie.

But just as Wade laid his list on the counter in front of Effie, the front door opened again. Wade wheeled to face Tank Crudup. He was caught now between the two Crudup brothers.

CHAPTER EIGHT

Tank Crudup crouched just inside the doorway, his eyes gleaming. 'I'm going to give you a choice, Vaun,' he said. 'Either draw or drag.'

'Why should I do either?' Wade demanded. 'We're both working for the same man.'

'Maybe you are,' Tank said. 'I work for myself. And I sure don't need your help.'

Wade shot a glance at Hobie. Cozetta was standing almost in front of him. She was looking more at him than at either Wade or Tank. Hobie wasn't going to find it easy to take a hand in this fight. So it was just between Wade and Tank.

'In that case,' Wade said slowly, 'I'll give you the same choice you're giving me.'

Wade waited. He didn't know how fast Tank Crudup was with a gun, but he had never seen a really big man like Tank who was lightning fast. Wade was; he worked long and hard on it.

Tank stood still, his legs spread to hold up his huge bulk. Wade expected him to make a move any second. But he hesitated, as if waiting for the exact psychological moment.

Wade slowly began to relax. Tank wasn't going to draw. His bluff had been called and he was backing down. Then suddenly a scream from Cozetta tore Wade's attention away from Tank.

He wheeled, whipping out his gun as he turned. He expected to see Hobie pulling his gun. Rut Hobie was still standing motionless beside Cozetta. From the back door, Luke Edris was dashing in, gun in hand, eyes flashing over the store. The first thing he saw was the speed of Wade's draw and he stopped dead in his tracks. His fingers spread, letting his gun clatter to the floor. Wade saw the astonishment on Hobie's face, too.

Wade wheeled back to Tank. This was just the diversion he needed to get his own gun in action. But he hadn't moved. Effie was standing behind the counter with her shotgun aimed at Tank. That shelf under the counter held more than sacks and boxes to put groceries in.

'Nobody's shooting up my store,' Effie said flatly.

Hobie whistled softly. 'I see why Uncle Jasper hired you, Vaun. You've got a quick hand.'

'What did you expect?' Wade said, hiding his own tension. 'I ought to ventilate one of you just to convince you not to be so reckless again.'

'You heard Effie,' Hobie said. 'She don't allow no shooting in here.'

'Fine with me,' Wade said. He turned to the counter as Tank slipped out the front door. Hobie collected his sack of groceries, then led Edris out the back way.

'Jasper Dovel sent me to town for this list of groceries, Mrs. Skarsten,' Wade said. 'Can you fill the order?'

'I'd rather fill him full of buckshot,' Effie said, glaring at the list. 'I see he wants his cornmeal so he can have his cornmeal mush for supper. Seems he's had it every night since he was a boy. Here, Cozetta, you get the sugar and beans. I'll get the cornmeal and these other things.'

Wade waited while the groceries were packed in sacks he could put in his saddle bags. Cozetta didn't look at him any of the time. He wondered what she was thinking. She had saved his life again. Edris would surely have shot him without warning if he hadn't been alerted. Likely Tank and Edris had seen him come into the store and planned this pincher move. That must have been what Tank had been waiting for. Cozetta's scream and Effie's shotgun had upset their plans.

As Wade picked up the sacks, he spoke to Cozetta. 'Seems I'm always thanking you for saving my neck. If it wasn't for you, I wouldn't be thanking anybody for anything now.'

'I just don't like to see anybody shot, especially in the back,' Cozetta said coolly.

Wade took his groceries and rode out of town. At the ranch, he was met in the yard by Jasper Dovel.

'What kind of scrape did you get into in town?' Dovel demanded.

Wade frowned. 'Scrape? What are you talking about?'

'Hobie and that sneak they call a hired hand, Luke Edris, came by here on their way home. Edris said he saw you draw. Never saw anything like it. Hobie acted like he wanted him to shut up. Who did you draw on? Edris?'

Wade's thoughts were spinning. The less said about that incident in the store, the better. He didn't want Dovel sending him out after the Crudups now. He'd pick his own time to go looking for them after he found out which one he wanted for the murder of Brent Runyan. If Dovel knew that the Crudups were trying to kill his gunman, he'd retaliate. Jasper Dovel was not one to wait for a fight to be brought to him.

'I just had to show Edris that I knew which end of a gun to point at a man,' Wade said. 'I didn't figure to impress him much.'

'You did, anyway,' Dovel said. 'I'm glad to know I didn't pick a bum steer when I sent for you.'

Wade said nothing. He realized that Dovel had begun having some doubts about him. Maybe the incident in the store would eliminate those doubts.

Taking the sacks out of the saddle bags, Wade headed for the house with them. 'I figured you wouldn't need me here tonight,' he said. 'I'm having supper in town.'

Dovel grunted. 'Fanny, is it? Don't let her talk your head off.'

Wade grinned. 'I'll keep one ear closed.'

The sun was almost to the horizon when Wade headed back for town. Deep twilight had settled down when he reined his horse up in front of Deuce Ulrich's little house a block east of the marshal's office. Fanny stepped to the door and invited him in.

Fanny dominated the conversation during the meal. Deuce sat glumly at the table and mowed away his supper. Wade had to admit that Fanny wasn't a bad cook. Her constant talking didn't help his nerves any, but he ignored it and watched Deuce. Fanny's steady chatter seemed to bother him more than it did Wade.

When supper was over, Deuce retired to a chair in the corner of the room, lit up his pipe and pretended to be deeply engrossed in a week-old newspaper. Wade went to the kitchen with Fanny and helped her with the dishes. He figured she wasn't going to show him that drawing of the man killed on the stage until she had finished her work.

With the dishes finished, Wade suggested that he'd like to see some more samples of her drawing.

'You mean that drawing I made of the marshal killed in the stage wreck?' Fanny said. 'Maybe that's what you came for instead of supper.'

Wade grinned. 'You saw how I ate.'

''I like a man who eats well,' Fanny said.

She brought out a big pad. Each sheet of paper had a drawing on it. Wade could see that Fanny had a natural talent for reproducing what she saw. There were a couple of scenes from along the creek. One was near the bluff below the Burdeens', close to the place where the stage had gone over. Wade recognized it immediately.

Then she flipped a sheet and there was the drawing of Wade Vaun. Wade caught his breath. A photographer couldn't have reproduced a much better likeness. If someone was sent here to check on the death of Wade Tillotson and saw that picture of the dead marshal, he'd know instantly that they had the wrong man.

'You couldn't spare that picture, could you?'

Fanny shook her head. 'Pa said I'm to keep it in case some of that marshal's relatives came to identify it. If you want a copy, I can make another one from this drawing.'

'I wouldn't ask you to do that,' Wade said hastily. 'I just saw the man that one time. But I'd recognize him, all right. Your drawings are good.'

After visiting for over an hour, Wade excused himself, saying that Dovel didn't want him gone from the ranch long at a time. He had the feeling that Fanny was sharper than she pretended to be. The longer he was exposed to her prying eyes, the more risk he was taking that she would see through his disguise.

Wade took his time going home. It was late when he put his horse away. He saw that the lamp was still burning in the living room. He found Jasper and his wife, Sarah, there along with their daughter, Maddie, and her husband.

One look at them and Wade knew all was not well.

'What's wrong?' he demanded.

'We're sick,' Mattie snapped. 'Can't you see that?'

'All of you?'

'Ain't nobody laughing, is there?' Cal Fenton said, groaning.

'What happened?' Wade asked, still bewildered.

'We don't know,' Maddie said. 'We've all got cramps. Maybe somebody tried to poison us.'

'Ride back to town and bring Doc Melton,' Dovel said.

'Where does he live?'

'First house you come to as you go into town,' Dovel said. 'He's not even a good horse doctor, but he's all we've got at Nevermore.' He groaned. 'Hurry up.'

Wade wheeled and went back to the corral and caught a fresh horse. As he saddled up, he tried to think how anyone could possibly have poisoned the whole family. It looked like poison, all right. Maddie and Cal Fenton were as sick as Jasper and Sarah Dovel.

Swinging on his horse, he kicked him into a gallop toward town. Suddenly it hit him. Effie Skarsten. She had said she wished she could fill Jasper Dovel full of buckshot instead of filling his grocery list. She must have put something in the groceries she put in that sack he'd brought out to the ranch this afternoon. If

Wade had eaten with the Dovels instead of visiting Fanny Ulrich for supper, he'd have been sick, too. Wade knew that the Dovels shared their groceries with Maddie and Cal Fenton. That would account for all of them being sick.

Wade stopped at the first house he came to and hammered on the door. A squinty-eyed old man opened the door after the third pounding.

'What's chawing on you?' he demanded angrily. 'Trying to knock my house down?'

'Jasper Dovel said for you to come out right away. He's sick. So's all the rest of his family.'

The man wiped a hand across his face. 'I ain't hankerin' for a ride this time of night. But I'll go. What's wrong with them?'

'I don't know,' Wade said. 'May be poisoned.'

The old man nodded and disappeared back into the house. Wade didn't wait for him. He mounted and rode on into town. Effie Skarsten had a little house directly behind her store and Wade stopped there. There was no light.

He hammered on Effie's door. She answered the knock much quicker than the horse doctor had.

'Oh, it's you,' she said, opening the door a crack so her lamp would throw a sliver of light on her visitor.

'What did you put in those groceries you sent out to Dovel's?' Wade demanded.

Effie eyed him suspiciously. 'What kind of a question is that?'

'A plain one. And I want a plain answer. Everyone out there is sick.'

'You ain't.'

'I had supper at Ulrich's,' Wade said. 'What did you put in those groceries?'

'Nothing that's going to kill anybody—worse luck. Just some calomel. They may think they're going to die, but they won't. They'll probably kill me, though.'

'Not if they don't figure out who did it,' Wade said.

'You're not going to tell them?'

'Why should I? I didn't get sick. Did you give some to the Crudups, too?'

Effie smiled, the first time he'd ever seen the scowl break away from her face. 'They both bought cornmeal. Calomel sifts into cornmeal so you can't see it or taste it. You're not going to tell?'

Wade shook his head. 'No. But they may figure it out just like I did.'

He turned back to his horse. Now that he knew what was the matter with the Dovel family, it struck him as ridiculously funny. If Effie got any satisfaction from what she had done, she had earned it after living in the shadow of Jasper Dovel's threats all these years.

He rode back up the creek, but he didn't stop at Dovel's. Instead, he rode on to the spot where he and Fanny had stopped the other day. Here he reined his horse into the creek and crossed to the north side. Fanny had said the Crudups lived just ahead. If they had gotten as heavy a dose of that calomel as the Dovels had, they wouldn't be paying much attention to any unwanted company. It could be the break Wade needed to look for Brent Runyan's pearl-handled revolver.

There was a lamp burning in the main room of the house as Wade approached. He rode into the yard cautiously. There might be a dog here. He'd seen a dog following Tank Crudup. But Tank didn't live here any more. Everything was quiet, so evidently neither Hobie nor Kate had a dog. That was all to the good.

Wade rode past the house and dismounted in the rear. The front room was lighted up. That would be where the sick ones would be gathered. Misery liked company, so they would likely all be together. Wade was depending on that and on the probability that they'd be so sick they wouldn't pay any attention to any accidental noise he happened to make.

Slipping up to the house, he found a window half open. He shoved it the rest of the way up and carefully climbed inside. He could hear voices and groans in the other room. Apparently the Crudups had had cornmeal mush for supper, too, a habit that both Jasper and Kate had probably carried with them from childhood.

Wade found himself in a bedroom. Cautiously he struck a match. The door into the other room was closed. So far he was lucky. Going to the bureau, he looked over everything on top. From the clothes strewn around the room, he knew he was in Kate's room. He wished it was Hobie's room. If that pearl-handled revolver was in the house, it would more than likely be in Hobie's possession.

Still, he might find something important in Kate's room. He couldn't afford to waste time. He didn't know how long his luck would hold out.

He slid open a bureau drawer and found nothing but a waddedup mass of clothes. Kate was anything but a neat housekeeper. The second drawer he opened squeaked a little as it came out. He had to strike another match as the one in his fingers burned down to the end. He listened for any sound of movement in the other room, but a groan was all he heard.

When the match flared up, light reflected from the handle of the pearl inlay on the revolver lying on top of the clothes in the drawer. That was Brent Runyan's revolver, all right. Hobie or Tank must have given it to Kate to keep for them.

He was just reaching for it when he heard the door behind him open. With a quick puff, he blew out the match.

'Who's in here?' Kate's shrill voice cut the

darkness like a knife.

Wade froze. If she had a gun, she'd shoot him down; he had no doubt about that.

CHAPTER NINE

'Who's there?' Kate half screamed. 'Speak up! Hobie, bring the lamp. I can't see nothing in here.'

A groan came from the other room, then Hobie's voice spoke weakly. 'Aw, Ma, forget it. If anybody intended to shoot you, he'd have done it by now.'

'Bring that lamp!' Kate screamed. 'You ain't that sick.'

'I am, too.' Hobie said.

Wade decided that Kate must not have her gun with her or she would have been using it by now, spraying the darkness with bullets. If he waited another minute, she'd find a gun, even in the dark.

Making a dive for the window, Wade got one foot through before Kate lunged at him. With his free foot, he met her charge and she grunted heavily as she ran into his boot. Before she could recover, Wade was through the window and running for his horse.

Behind him he heard Kate screaming and swearing. Then a light appeared at the window and a shotgun exploded. But Wade was already mounted and out of range. The noise of the gun seemed to put wings on his horse's feet, and within seconds Wade was down in the creek valley, heading east.

Once out of sight and hearing of the Crudup place, Wade eased back on the reins. Kate apparently wasn't as sick as Hobie and Luke Edris. Maybe she hadn't eaten as much of the cornmeal mush for supper.

Wade had found the pearl handled revolver and that convinced him that one of the Crudups had surely killed Brent Runyan. But which one? If Wade had found it in Hobie's room, he would have felt certain Hobie was the one, certain enough that he might have arrested him now. But he had found it in Kate's room. Did that mean that Tank had killed Brent and had given the gun to Kate when he moved to the Runyan place? Or maybe Kate had seen the gun and demanded it for herself. In that case, she could have gotten it from either Tank or Hobie. Wade didn't doubt that Kate could take anything she wanted from her boys. He wondered what would happen to Hobie for not bringing the lamp immediately when Kate called for it. Sickness would be no excuse in Kate's eyes.

From what Wade had heard Dovel say, he approved and might even have called for Brent Runyan's murder. But Wade was beginning to see a pattern here that Jasper didn't control. It had been to the Crudups' advantage to get rid of Brent, too, and they might have done it strictly for selfish reasons. Now with Tank on the Runyan place, the Crudups had Jasper Dovel surrounded.

If Kate had any designs on Dovel's kingship of this valley, she would have to be in a position to keep him hemmed in. She was in that position now. Jasper Dovel's cowboys were not real fighting men. They might fight if Dovel ordered them to, but they would be outgunned whenever they met up individually with one of the Crudups. Many of them would quit if it came to a showdown.

If the Crudups had such a plan, the only real obstacle in the path of its success was Wade. They thought he was a hired killer. If they knew he was a marshal, they'd be even more intent on getting rid of him. His draw against Luke Edris at the store had been a lucky break for him. They knew now that he was fast with a gun and that would command more respect. It might also earn him a bullet in the back.

As Wade rode into the ranch yard, he saw the little man he had roused out of bed coming out of the house. Wade intercepted him.

'How are they doing?'

'As well as anyone can who's just taken a quart of castor oil,' the little man said. 'What did they get hold of?'

'Calomel,' Wade said. 'I don't know much about that stuff, but I have it on good authority that's what they got.'

'Did you give it to them?'

Wade shook his head vigorously. 'No, I didn't. And I won't tell you who did. Do you need to tell them exactly what's wrong with them?'

The little man thought about it then shook his head. 'I reckon not. The medicine I gave them is as good as anything they can take. If it's calomel, they sure got plenty of it.'

He went on to his horse and swung up into the saddle with an effort. 'I'm too old to be riding around like this at night,' he said and nudged his horse out of the yard at a walk.

Wade went into the house and straight on to his room. He'd be in the clear as long as those who were sick didn't jump to the same conclusion that the little horse doctor had, that he had given it to them. It might look suspicious to them when they thought about his invitation to eat at Ulrich's the very night they got the doctored food.

Morning found the whole family weak and grumpy but no longer afraid of dying. Maddie was furious.

'Somebody poisoned us,' she half screamed. 'It had to be Effie. She put something in our cornmeal. She has always hated us. This was just the chance she was waiting for.'

Wade didn't say anything. He went to the kitchen and found some bread and cold meat, and ate his breakfast. Nobody else was interested in food this morning.

By noon the sickness had worn off, but Maddie was getting more furious by the minute. All her anger was directed at Effie Skarsten.

'Pa, are you going to town and settle with Effie?' Maddie demanded during the afternoon.

'I ain't going nowhere I don't have to go right now,' Jasper said weakly.

'Then I'll do it myself,' she said.

'Now what are you going to do, Madeline?' Sarah asked.

'I'm going to kill her,' Maddie said. 'She deserves it.'

'She's had enough hard luck with Herman getting killed in that stage wreck,' Sarah said.

'She didn't need to poison us because of that. We didn't do it.'

'She may think we did,' Sarah said.

'Don't pester the girl,' Jasper said sternly to Sarah. 'She's right. Effie had no right to poison us.' He glared at Cal Fenton sitting dejectedly on a chair near the corner. 'What are you going to do about it?'

Fenton looked up, obviously startled. 'What can I do?'

'If you were half a man, you'd do what Maddie is planning on doing. In the Dovel family, we don't let our women do our fighting for us.'

'Just doesn't seem like a thing a man should fight about,' Fenton said.

‘Let him alone, Pa,’ Maddie said. ‘He wouldn’t fight a sick lizard. I’ll take care of things.’

Jasper glared at Wade. ‘I hired you to do my fighting. You take care of it.’

Wade glared back at the old man. ‘I don’t fight women,’ he said.

‘All right,’ Jasper grumbled. ‘Maybe it takes a woman to deal with a woman. She’s all yours, Maddie.’

Wade went outside.

This presented a new problem. He couldn’t let Maddie kill Effie, and she’d do just that if she wasn’t stopped. He had told Jasper he didn’t fight women, but he had a feeling he might be fighting Maddie before this was over.

He got his horse and saddled him, not even asking Dovel’s permission to leave. As he rode out of the yard, he saw Maddie coming out of her little house, a gun belt strapped around her waist. She was still pretty weak, but apparently she felt she was strong enough to handle Effie Skarsten. Her anger was at its peak right now.

Wade touched his horse into a gallop. If he warned Effie about Maddie, she could be ready. He recalled how Effie had held Tank Crudup at the end of her shotgun yesterday. She could likely take care of herself if she was looking for trouble.

Wade had every intention of riding directly to Effie’s store and warning her that Maddie was coming. But as he rode down the main street, he saw a man come out of the marshal's office. He stared hard at the man for a moment, then reined sharply off the street into the alley between Prandall's Hardware and the vacant building just to the south.

The man coming out of the marshal's office was Ike Yancey, the sheriff over in Claymore County just to the east. Yancey had been the last man Wade had seen before he boarded the stage to Nevermore. It was like Yancey to come and check up on him because he hadn't heard from him since he left Blue Springs. Wade should have sent word to Yancey what he was doing.

Now he had to get hold of Yancey and find out just how much he had told Deuce Ulrich. He didn't dare meet Yancey face to face on the street. Yancey would surely say or do something that would tell everyone watching that they knew each other and were friends. Wade Vaun, the gunman, would not have known Yancey and he certainly would not have been his friend.

Wade waited until Yancey had ridden down to the livery barn and turned in. Apparently he was planning on staying in Nevermore for a while. Wade dismounted and tied his horse behind the vacant building, then ran behind Prandall's store to the side street. He ignored the possibility that Prandall might be hiding in his store just waiting for an opportunity to kill one of the men he was after.

Wade crossed the side street and climbed into the corral behind the livery barn. The few horses there ran to the far side. Wade crossed to the front of the corral and waited till Ike Yancey came out of the barn.

When Yancey was even with the corral on his way back toward the hotel, Wade called softly to him. Yancey wheeled, his hand touching his gun.

'Don't get jumpy,' Wade said softly.

Yancey relaxed when he recognized Wade. 'Trying to keep out of sight?' he asked, turning to look back down the street.

'Exactly. Meet me behind the empty store, second building down the street on your left.'

'I'll be there,' Yancey agreed and walked on down the street toward Prandall's.

Wade ducked back across the corral and climbed the fence then crossed the street and went to his horse behind the vacant building. In less than a minute, Ike Yancey joined him there.

'I figured you were dead when I didn't hear from you,' Yancey said. 'How are things?'

'I would be dead if they knew who I was around here,' Wade said. 'They think I'm Jasper Dovel's hired killer.'

Yancey rubbed his chin thoughtfully. 'That's what they did think.'

'Did you tell them who I am?'

'No,' Yancey said quickly. 'But they may figure it out in a hurry.'

'What did you tell them?' Wade asked. 'I thought Deuce Ulrich would tell you the marshal who was on the stage was dead.'

'He did tell me that,' Yancey admitted. 'But then he wanted me to identify the dead man.'

'With a picture?'

Yancey nodded. 'How did you know?'

'I saw that picture. Fanny showed it to me. That is a perfect picture of the man who was killed when the stage went over the bluff. I knew they had meant to get me, so I changed identifications with him. That's why everybody thought the marshal was killed.'

'And you've been in Dovel's house, acting like his hired killer?'

Wade nodded. 'I've been learning things it might have taken me weeks to find out any other way.'

'I'm sorry I messed up your plans,' Yancey said. 'But I was really down in the mouth when the marshal showed me the things they took off the dead man. They were yours, all right. Then I saw that picture and I knew that wasn't you. I should have guessed what you had done.'

'Don't blame yourself,' Wade said, trying to plan his next move.

'Do you know yet who killed Brent Runyan?' Yancey asked.

Wade shook his head. 'Not for sure. I'm positive it was one of the Crudups, but I don't know whether it was Tank or Hobie. I should have arrested one of them, anyway. If he was the wrong one, I think he'd have squealed to save his own hide. I've got them tagged as being that selfish.'

'Nobody but Ulrich knows that the dead man was not the marshal,' Yancey said. 'If we tell him to keep it quiet, maybe you can go on with your masquerade.'

'No chance,' Wade said. 'Deuce is Jasper Dovel's righthand man. He'll break his neck getting to Dovel with this information.'

Wade realized that he was in more danger now than he had been at any time since he'd arrived in Nevermore. Even Deuce himself would try to kill him now.

CHAPTER TEN

A horse charged up the street out in front of the building and Wade suddenly remembered Maddie Fenton and her determination to kill Effie.

'I've got a woman fight to stop,' he said suddenly. 'Watch out for that marshal. He knows Dovel doesn't want any lawmen here, and he'll do anything to keep on the good side of Dovel.'

He ran up the little alley between the two buildings to the street. Maddie was dismounting in front of Effie Skarsten's store.

Wade could see that the ride had drained much of her strength. But she still had strength enough to handle her gun. Like a wounded rattler, she was deadly as long as she could strike.

Running as hard as he could, Wade raced past the vacant building to the door of Skarsten's Grocery. Maddie was already inside. Slamming open the door, he saw Maddie with her gun in her hand and he charged into her, knocking the gun to the floor.

Maddie stumbled and when she caught herself, she wheeled on Wade with all the fury of a wildcat.

'You blooming idiot!' she yelled. 'Watch where you're going.'

'I was watching,' Wade said.

'What's going on?' Effie demanded, grabbing her shotgun from under the counter.

'Maddie figured you put something in that cornmeal,' Wade explained. 'She was all primed to kill you for it.'

'Well now, it might take more than a little spitfire like her to do that,' Effie said. 'Kick that gun over here where I can get it. I can handle things now.'

Wade agreed that Effie was right. She could handle things all right as long as she had both her shotgun and Maddie's pistol.

Stepping back outside, Wade turned toward the marshal's office next to the grocery store.

He had to get hold of Deuce Ulrich before he ran to Jasper Dovel with the news that the dead man was not Marshal Wade Tillotson.

Back inside the store, he heard Maddie screaming vengeance against both Effie and Wade. That shotgun Effie was holding was all that was preventing violence now. Maddie became as wild as a wounded bear when her temper got out of control, which was quite often. Wade would have to be on the lookout for Maddie if he ran into her again.

He turned in to the marshal's office but it was empty. Wade took a quick look in the jail behind the office. Deuce wasn't there, either. He must have headed out for Dovel's ranch already.

Wade went back to the street. What few things he had were out at Dovel's ranch, but if Deuce got out there before he did, he wouldn't dare go in after them.

Maybe Deuce hadn't left town yet. Wade ran down the side street to Ulrich's home a block east. He didn't stop at the house but went on around to the barn behind the house. It seemed like a logical guess that the marshal would keep his horse there. However, he found only one horse there and that horse was roaming around inside the barn as though he owned it all.

Turning back to the house, he rapped sharply on the door. Fanny came to answer it.

'Where's Deuce?' Wade asked.

Fanny shrugged. 'I suppose he's in his office.'

'Doesn't he keep his horse in his barn?'

Fanny shook her head. 'Pa lets me keep my horse there. He has his horse at the livery barn. Says it's just as close to his work and somebody always has him fed and ready to go whenever he needs him."

Wade turned back toward town. 'Thanks, Fanny. I've got some business to take care of.'

He glanced back once. Fanny was standing in the doorway watching him. He wasn't liable to be seeing Fanny again. The logical thing for him to do now was to get out of the country before the combined forces of Jasper Dovel, the Crudups, and Deuce Ulrich caught up with him. He wished he had arrested Hobie Crudup when he had the chance last night while the family was sick.

He thought of Brent Runyan's place, which he owned now, and the impulse to stay and fight for what was his swept over him. The odds were all against him. But if he ran, he'd show no more backbone than the homesteaders who had already run before the threat of Jasper Duel.

Reaching the livery barn, he hurried inside. In the half light of the barn's interior, he saw the boy who apparently worked here most of the time but he didn't see Deuce Ulrich.

'Looks like you've been pushing on the reins,' Ike Yancey said from the shadows of one of the empty stalls.

'I have been,' Wade said as Yancey stepped out where he could see him. 'Thought I might catch Deuce before he left town.'

Yancey nodded and went outside, motioning for Wade to follow him. 'He was here,' he said once they were out of earshot of the boy. 'I talked to him, being careful he didn't try to slicker me. But he had only one thing in mind, to get out to Dovel's with the news that the dead man wasn't the marshal.'

'Figured on that,' Wade said. 'How long has he been gone?'

'Only a couple of minutes,' Yancey said. 'But he won't get to Dovel's for a while. I told him somebody from down river had been here looking for him. Said his daughter was down there and wanted to see him quick.'

'He believed you?'

'Seemed to. I took a chance that he hadn't seen his daughter since I'd been with him at his house, which was a while ago. By the time he finds out that's a false alarm and gets back to Dovel's, you'll have time to get out there and clear out your stuff.'

'You were thinking ahead of me,' Wade said. 'I thought I'd have to leave the few things I have out there. You'd better get out of town yourself. Dovel doesn't want any law in this valley except his own.'

'Meaning Deuce Ulrich?'

Wade nodded. 'That's it, Jasper Dovel's law.

Mrs. Prandall called it the law of the lawless.'

'I'll have to agree with that,' Yancey said. 'I think I'll stick around for a while. Like to see what happens. Are you going to make any arrests before you leave?'

'Not sure I'm going to leave,' Wade said. 'I own Brent Runyan's place, you know. It's a good place; I'd like to live there.'

'In this valley?' Yancey asked in surprise. 'How would you get along with neighbors like Jasper Dovel and the Crudups?'

'At least one of the Crudups may be spending some time elsewhere if I can prove he killed Brent.'

'First you've got to arrest him.' Yancey scratched his head. 'I'm going to stick around. This could get interesting.'

'What about your own county?'

'My deputy can handle things there. I told him I might be gone a few days.'

'You're buying into a fast game with stacked cards.' Wade warned.

'Won't be the first time,' Yancey said. 'I reckon you're going to need a hand. Are you opposed to having help?'

'I wouldn't ask anybody to help me,' Wade said. 'But I'm not fool enough to turn down any help that's offered, either.'

'When are you going to make your arrest?'

'First, I want to get my stuff from Dovel's,' Wade said. 'Then I'll see about arresting one or both of the Crudups.'

'I think you'll have plenty of time to get to Dovel's ahead of Deuce,' Yancey said. 'I want you to meet someone I've been talking to. Could be he'll be some help to us, too.'

Wade frowned as Yancey turned back toward the barn. 'That boy?' he asked. 'He's scared of his own shadow.'

'Not the boy,' Yancey said. Wade followed Yancey into the barn. He stopped just inside, his hand involuntarily dropping to his gun. Standing next to the boy was George Prandall. But Prandall showed none of the killing rage he had turned on Wade the last time they had met.

'You know George Prandall, don't you?'

'Met him once,' Wade said warily.

'I've been talking to him while I was waiting for you to show up. I figured you'd come here after you stopped that woman war you were talking about.'

'He tells me you're really a deputy U.S. marshal,' Prandall said.

Wade looked at the hardware owner closely. He wasn't crazy, that was sure, in spite of the word that Deuce had brought to Jasper Dovel.

'I thought you were after my hide,' Wade said.

'That was when I thought you were Jasper Dovel's hired killer,' Prandall explained. 'I don't reckon you were to blame for Nancy's and Sue's deaths and if you're not working for Dovel, you've got to be against him. There are only two sides in this country. Looks like we may be on the same one.'

Wade looked from Prandall to Yancey, who was grinning at him.

'Agree?' Yancey asked.

Wade nodded. 'I guess so. I figure I'm lucky I didn't run into him before you talked to him.'

'He did seem all set to do you in along with about a dozen others,' Yancey said. 'But if he works with us, he'll have to curb his killer instincts.'

'I'm not keen on doing the killing myself,' Prandall said. 'I just want to see them dead.'

'Our job is to arrest them,' Yancey said. 'Let the law punish them.'

'Won't get much punishment in this county,' Prandall said disgustedly, shaking his head.

'I've got to get my stuff from Dovel's before Deuce gets out there,' Wade said.

'We'll stay here at the barn,' Yancey said, 'until you get back. The kid has promised not to tell anyone we're here.'

'Think you can trust him?'

Yancey looked sharply at the boy. 'I think so. Isn't that right, kid?'

The boy was so scared he stuttered. 'Sure is. I won't tell nobody you're here.'

'Better get going, Wade,' Yancey said.

Wade went back to the rear of the vacant building along the main street where he had left his horse. Mounting, he reined the horse into the street and put him to a gallop toward

Dovel's ranch.

The sun was almost down when he left town. It was gone before he reached the ranch. In the twilight, he checked for Deuce's horse but didn't see it. Apparently the ruse Yancey had pulled on Deuce had kept him from reaching Dovel's yet.

Wade didn't ride directly to the house. There was always the chance that Deuce had crossed up Yancey and ridden straight out here or had met someone who would bring the word to Jasper Dovel. In that case, Dovel would likely shoot Wade on Sight without asking questions.

Wade reined up behind the barn and dismounted. In the deepening darkness, he slipped around the corral and headed for the rear of the house. His room was a back one and he remembered leaving the window open this morning to air the room out. He should be able to get in there and collect his things and get out without the family knowing he had even been here.

The window was still open and Wade climbed throught it, being as quiet as possible. Quickly he went around the room, feeling for things he couldn't see in the dark.

Most of the things he called his own had really belonged to Wade Vaun. Jasper had sent his foreman to bring them out from Deuce Ulrich's office where they had been taken from the wreck. Andy Kent had naturally brought

Vaun's things.

Wade had about finished collecting what he wanted to save when he heard a horse charge into the front yard. He was sure that would be Deuce Ulrich. He should get out now, but curiosity held him. What would Deuce tell Jasper? Had Deuce figured out that if the dead man wasn't the U.S. marshal, then the man pretending to be Wade Vaun probably was?

The front door banged open and voices started chattering. Wade distinguished Maddie Fenton's voice among them, sharp and shrill. Deuce was trying to talk, too. Then Jasper gravelly voice cut through all the chatter and silenced it.

'Let Deuce talk. He acts like he has a polecat by the tail.'

'I have,' Deuce said. 'You know that marshal that was killed in the stage wreck? Well, he wasn't killed.'

'What do you mean?' Jasper bellowed. 'You buried him, didn't you?'

'I buried the dead man, yes. But it wasn't the marshal.'

'Who says so?'

'Ike Yancey, the sheriff from Claymore County. He was over to see what happened to the marshal. I showed him the picture Fanny drew of the dead man. He says that ain't Tillotson.'

Jasper snorted. 'Fanny probably just can't draw worth a whoop.'

'She can, too,' Ulrich shouted. 'Everybody recognizes her pictures.'

Silence settled over the front of the house. Finally Jasper spoke, quietly now.

'If that wasn't Tillotson, then who was it?'

'Could it have been Wade Vaun?' Maddie asked. 'Your gun slinger?'

'Couldbe,' Jasper said. 'But if it was, then who is the fellow who's passing off as Vaun?'

'The marshal,' Maddie said, her voice rising in excitement.

'Where is he now?' Jasper demanded, his voice rising, too.

'He was in town a while ago,' Maddie said. 'Slammed into me to keep me from shooting Effie for poisoning us. I should have known right then that he wasn't who he's been pretending to be. Vaun wouldn't have stopped me from shooting Effie.'

'How long ago did you find this out, Deuce?' Jasper demanded.

'Not too long,' Deuce said uneasily. 'I was told Fanny was down by Burdeens' and had sent word for me to come down there. I went but she wasn't there. She was home.'

'Who told you that?' Jasper screamed.

'Yancey, that sheriff,' Deuce said.

'Your orders are to get word to me immediately if you find out anything like this!'

'I came as soon as I knew Fanny was all right,' Deuce insisted.

'I'll give a thousand dollars to the man who

gets that marshal!' Jasper roared.

'I'm going to see if he's been here to get his stuff,' Maddie said suddenly.

Wade scrambled for the window but he knew he'd never make it. Maddie was coming on the run. He had waited too long.

CHAPTER ELEVEN

Wade had just reached the window when he heard Maddie hit the partition door. He had an innate inhibition against shooting at a woman, but he had to stop Maddie. He knew that she wouldn't hesitate to shoot at him.

Swinging up his gun, he fired a shot into the top of the door, well above the level of Maddie's head. He heard her scream but the door didn't open. Wade swung his legs over the windowsill and dropped to the ground. Within seconds now, he expected someone to barge into that bedroom or around the corner of the house.

Wade ran in a crouch, offering as small a target as possible without hindering his speed. He was almost to the corral when a gun roared from the house. He didn't slacken his pace or attempt to return the fire.

Diving around the corner of the corral, he dashed for the rear of the barn. There he swung on his horse and spurred him into a run toward the river.

Several shots searched for him in the growing darkness, but none found their mark. At the edge of the water willows, he swung his horse upstream. But once hidden from the house by the willows and the creek bank, he turned his horse downstream.

Splashing across the stream, Wade rode along the creek bank till he came to a deep draw that cut into the creek from the north. There were some bushes in the bottom of the draw and Wade found the densest thicket and turned into it.

He considered riding on to the livery barn in town to meet Ike Yancey and George Prandall. But town would be one of the first places Jasper Dovel would have Deuce and his men look, unless they fell for his ruse of turning upstream. He couldn't depend on that.

Dismounting, he tied his horse to one of the bushes, loosened the cinch, then laid down to get what little rest he could. He imagined that Dovel would spread his men out in a search for him. He had to be ready to run if they found him.

But the night passed quietly. Only once did Wade hear anything to rouse his suspicions. A rider passed to the south along the creek but he didn't turn up the draw and Wade kept quiet, holding a hand over the nose of his horse to keep him from whinnying a welcome to the other horse.

With the first light of dawn, Wade tightened the cinch on the saddle and mounted, riding back to the creek and heading downstream. As he passed the Runyan place, he noticed the light in the window. Apparently Tank and his wife, Tunie, were having breakfast. It reminded Wade that he hadn't had anything to eat since yesterday noon.

When he reached town, he rode up to the corral behind the livery barn and dismounted, hurrying to the back door of the barn. The door was shut but not locked and Wade rolled it open far enough to get inside.

As he moved down the wide alley between the stalls, he looked for the ladder leading into the loft. Yancey was probably up there. But he was surprised when the sheriff suddenly appeared in front of him, stepping out from an empty stall.

'What happened to you?' Yancey asked in a hoarse whisper. 'We thought you'd be back last night.'

'Had a close call at Dovel's,' Wade said. 'Figured they'd be sure to look for me here in town so I stayed out along the creek.'

'That explains the ruckus here last night. Two men came storming through the barn, looking in every stall. Even climbed up in the haymow.'

'Did they find you?'

Yancey nodded. 'Sure. But the kid told them I was a drifter just spending the night. They didn't ask me any questions. They seemed to know exactly who they were looking for.'

'Probably did,' Wade said. 'Me. Where's Prandall?'

'He went back to his store to sleep. He said he'd be here early this morning. What's your plan now? Arrest the Crudups?'

'Maybe,' Wade said. 'But we're going to have to be mighty careful. Dovel has a lot of men combing the country looking for me. Dovel doesn't like having somebody make him look like a fool, and he'll think that's what I've done.'

Yancey grinned. 'I guess you have, at that. I'd like to meet this Jasper Dovel. I've heard a lot about him.'

'Right now you'd better hope you don't meet him.'

The sun was coming up when George Prandall slipped quietly into the back of the barn. Yancey greeted him then turned back to Wade.

'If we have to lay low, just where do you suggest we do it?'

'Out at the place I bought,' Wade said, then told Yancey and Prandall about the tunnel Brent Runyan had dug as a means of escape from his house in case he was trapped there.

'Tank Crudup and his wife have moved into the house,' Wade said. 'We'll hope they haven't found that tunnel yet.'

'You expect us to live in that tunnel?'

Prandall asked.

'For a while,' Wade said. 'I've got an idea how to get Tank and Tunie out of the house. Then we'll have a decent place to live.'

'Let's try it,' Yancey said.

Yancey and Prandall saddled horses and led them outside. Wade went back out through the corral to his horse. The town was just beginning to stir into life when the three rode across the bridge to the north side of the creek. There Wade led the way upstream.

Close to the Runyan place, Wade reined up to study the area. The house sat back from the creek a ways and the barn and corral were to the west of the house. A shed stood east of the house. Wade could understand why Brent had decided on the tunnel. From the low bluff along the creek, he only had to dig straight back until he got under the house, then come up into it. The tunnel floor shouldn't have much of a slope to it.

'Tank's horse is gone,' Wade said after a while, 'but he may not be far away. We can hide our horses in those cottonwoods down there. Then we'll walk to the tunnel mouth.'

The others nodded silently. With the horses carefully hidden in the trees, the three slipped through the water willows to the mouth of the tunnel Wade had located the other day. Moving some of the tree limbs, Wade revealed the mouth of the tunnel, big enough for a man to get into but not stand upright.

‘Going to be cramped in there if we have to stay long,’ Yancey said.

‘Don’t expect to stay there long,’ Wade said.

Once the three were inside the tunnel, Wade reached back and arranged the tree limbs to cover the opening so no casual passerby would see it.

As he led the way up the tunnel, he found that the ceiling rose. Apparently Brent had made the mouth of the tunnel smaller than the tunnel itself so it could be more easily hidden. A shaft of light came down from the ceiling up ahead. Wade paused under the little hole in the tunnel roof.

‘A horse’s hoof must have broken through there,’ he said, looking up through the hole.

He explained about Tunie’s fear of ghosts and outlined his plan to get rid of Tank and Tunie. The others agreed that the plan was worth a try. Anything was better than trying to live here in this tunnel indefinitely.

Wade followed the tunnel until it ended in a straight wall. A short ladder stood against the tunnel’s end. Wade struck a match and looked up. A trap door was above his head. He wondered if Tank and Tunie had found that.

Above them, Wade heard footsteps. ‘Sounds like a woman walking,’ he whispered. ‘That would be Tunie. I’m going to see what’s going on.’

Slowly climbing the ladder, Wade reached above his head and pushed on the trap door. It gave without a sound. Wade wouldn't have been surprised to have found it locked from above. He discovered quickly that a rug covered it. But as he lifted it, the edge of the rug lifted, too, and Wade could see under it into the room.

A woman was standing at the far side of the room, peeling some potatoes at a bench. That would be Tunie Crudup, Wade guessed. He had never seen her before. Lowering the door until only a slit remained, he spoke in a strained falsetto voice:

'What are you doing in my house?'

Tunie screamed and wheeled around, then stood still as if paralyzed.

'I am Brent Runyan,' Wade intoned. 'What are you doing in my house?'

Tunie screeched again and wheeled toward the door. As she slammed through it into the yard, Wade pushed the trap door the rest of the way up and climbed into the room. Yancey and Prandall followed him. Wade went to the window to look for Tunie. She was running pell mell down the hill toward the creek, waving her arms and screaming. Wade saw Tank then, riding toward her from across the creek.

'We'll have to get back down in the tunnel,' Wade warned. 'She's bringing Tank.'

'If she comes back, I don't figure she'll be doing the bringing,' Yancey said, grinning.

Wade had to agree with that. He looked

around the room. The trap door was right in the very corner of the kitchen where few people would either step on it or see it. A small rug was thrown over it, barely covering the edge.

Looking out the window again, Wade saw that Tank and Tunie were arguing, waving their arms like windmills in a high wind. He could guess what they were saying. Tank apparently won the argument for they came back toward the house, Tank leading his horse, Tunie coming with great reluctance.

'Time to play like gophers again,' Wade said and lifted the trap door.

After Prandall and Yancey had gone down the ladder, Wade started down then lowered the trap door, making sure the rug was in position to slide over the crack around the door when it was closed.

Above them, Wade heard Tank's heavy footsteps as he stamped around the kitchen then swore at Tunie who apparently had stayed in the other room. Wade heard another sound he didn't like, the sniffing of a dog near the trap door. That dog would find things that Tank or Tunie would never notice. But apparently the two were not interested in the dog and what he was finding.

'I'm going to town,' Tank roared above Tunie's frightened arguments. 'You can stay here and play with your ghosts.'

'Oh, no, I won't!' Tunie screamed. 'I'm

going with you.'

The sounds faded and, after a long silence, Wade pushed up the door a trifle. The room was empty and he climbed into the kitchen again, holding the door for the others. Looking out the window, Wade saw Tank and Tunie riding toward town, half a mile away, a big hound trailing the horses.

'We need this house to ourselves,' Wade said. 'So let's figure how we're going to get Tank and Tunie out.'

'No problem with Tunie,' Yancey said. 'She's seen enough of this house right now.'

'Let's give her another reason for getting out,' Wade said. His eye fell on a small roll of smooth wire that Tank had apparently been using to wire a broken chair together. 'Wonder what a real visible ghost would do for Tunie. If she runs fast enough, Tank will have to go along.'

'You tell us what you want done and we'll get busy.' Prandall said.

'Nail a stick across the end of that broom handle,' Wade told Prandall. 'Ike, help me string this wire from the corner of the room down to this door.'

Yancey looked puzzled until he saw Wade hold the wire up to the ceiling in the corner above the trap door then slope it down to the door jamb so there was a good angle. He stretched two wires here a few inches apart. Then he hung the broom between the wires, suspended on the cross stick that Prandall had nailed to the handle. Tying a piece of string he found on the table to the broom, he ran it down to the trap door. By releasing the string slowly, the broom glided down the sloping wires toward the partition doorway. Satisfied, Wade pulled the broom back to the top of the wire then brought a sheet from the bedroom and draped it over the broom.

'Now that should look like a ghost, don't you think?'

Yancey grinned. 'It will when it starts moving toward that door.'

'We didn't get that fixed any too soon,' Prandall said from the window. 'Here they come back from town.'

'Let's get back in the hole and see if this thing will work,' Wade said.

The three got down the ladder again and Wade paid out the string and watched the ghost slide down the wires. Climbing back into the kitchen, he pushed the broom back to the top of the wires then went down the ladder, using a stick to keep the trap door from closing completely. This crack let him see into the room and also allowed the string to move freely.

Wade heard the argument between Tank and Tunie before they got in the house. Tunie didn't want to come in and Tank was swearing and ridiculing her for being such a coward. The dog, a big hunting hound, came in ahead of them.

The hound spotted the slightly open trap door before he saw the ghost hanging on the wires in the corner. He began a terrific roar, barking as though he had treed a bear. Tank hurried toward the kitchen, pushing Tunie ahead of him. She was screaming that she wouldn't go, but was being propelled into the kitchen like a leaf in a high wind.

It was so dark in the kitchen that anyone coming in from outside would have trouble seeing much at first. All Wade wanted them to see now was that white ghost moving down toward them.

As Tunie was pushed into the kitchen, Wade paid out the string and the ghost began moving slowly down the wires toward the partition doorway. Tunie's scream was the nearest thing to pure terror that Wade had ever heard. Even above that scream and the baying of the hound, he heard Tank gasp. Somehow Wade had to scare them out of here before Tank's reasoning told him this had to be a trick.

The dog was moving closer to the trap door, barking and growling as if ready to attack. So far, neither Tank nor Tunie was paying any attention to the dog. All they could see was that ghost moving down toward them.

The dog had his nose near the crack in the trap door now, within inches of Wade's face, barking furiously. Tank was sure to notice soon. Wade sucked in his break then gave one loud 'Woof' at the dog. The hound almost turned a backward flipflop getting away from the trap door. Wade thought that he wouldn't give much for a hunting dog with that kind of bravery.

Tunie screamed even louder, apparently thinking the new noise had come from the ghost. Even Tank retreated a step, shoved back by Tunie's frantic pushing.

The hound was looking for an exit and the only one he could see was the tunnel made by Tunie's and Tank's legs in the doorway. He charged for that tunnel only to find that the tunnel walls shifted at the last second and he slammed into Tunie's legs. The hound, though small in courage, was big in size and he catapulted Tunie into Tank just behind her.

Tank lost his balance and Tunie, Tank, and the hound became one wild, scrambling mass on the floor. Wade wasn't sure whether Tunie or the hound was more frightened. Her screams and the wild yips of the hound filled the room with bedlam. Wade was so fascinated by the sight that he almost forgot to pay out the string, letting the ghost slide slowly down the wires.

Tank, swearing shrilly, finally rolled free of the tangled mass of clawing hands, paws, and feet and jerked out his gun. He fired at the ghost but it kept coming at the same pace, slow and unstoppable. Frantically Tank emptied his gun—but still the ghost kept coming. What little courage Tank still had fled, and he scrambled to his feet, his terrified yells mingled with the screams of his wife and the continued yowling of the dog.

Tunie got untangled from the hound and tried to beat the dog to the door, but the hound had one-track mind and it was set on the door, too. The dog shot through the gap into the yard ahead of Tunie, but she was only a step behind. Tank's ponderous footsteps shook the house as he charged through the door in the wake of his wife's flight.

Suddenly all was quiet inside the house.

CHAPTER TWELVE

Wade pushed the trap door open and climbed into the kitchen, confident that they'd seen the last of Tank and Tunie in this house. The other two men scrambled up after Wade.

'You saw all the fun,' Yancey complained. 'That must have been some sight, judging from what I could hear.'

'It was,' Wade said. 'Especially when that hound slammed into Tunie and Tank in the doorway.'

George Prandall hurried to the window as soon as he reached the kitchen floor. 'Look at that,' he said. 'They've spooked their horses and now they're trying to catch them.'

Wade grinned as he stood behind Prandall and watched Tank and Tunie trying to catch their horses. Tunie kept flipping her head back as if she expected to see the ghost coming after her. Wade didn't see the dog at all.

'I doubt if they'll be back,' Yancey said.

'I think we can live here in peace now,' Wade agreed.

'What happens if we do have company?' Prandall asked.

'We'll duck down into our den like prairie dogs,' Wade said.

Prandall stood at the window and watched the two running after their horses. 'I wonder if they're out of rifle range,' he muttered.

'What difference does that make?' Wade asked. 'They're not going to do any more shooting. Tank tried to kill the ghost and when he couldn't, he'd had enough. He won't try again.'

'I wasn't thinking about Tank doing the shooting,' Prandall said.

'You don't have a rifle here,' Yancey said.

Prandall turned back from the window. 'I know. If I had, I'd give it a try.'

'To get Tank?' Wade asked.

Prandall nodded. 'He helped crowd that stage over the bluff and kill Nancy and Sue. Him and Hobie and Luke Edris. I snooped around until I found out that much.'

Yancey shook his head. 'Killing them won't bring back your wife and daughter.'

'They're not going to run free after what they did,' Prandall said, his face clouding like a threatening sky. 'This earth ain't big enough for them and me.'

'Better let the law take care of them,' Yancey said.

Prandall looked at Wade. 'I wish I'd had the chance you had. I'd have taken care of Tank when he came in that door.'

Wade realized that Prandall was as determined as ever to avenge the deaths of his wife and daughter. The same inner rage that had made Deuce Ulrich think he was crazy still drove him. Nothing was really changed except that Wade was no longer on Prandall's death list.

'Better let Ike and me take care of them,' Wade said.

'Why?' Prandall asked. 'They didn't kill your family.'

'They almost killed me,' Wade said.

'Then you ought to be out to get them,' Prandall said matter-of-factly. 'An eye for an eye, you know.'

'We ought to bring our horses closer,' Yancey said. 'We might need them in a hurry.'

'You're right,' Wade agreed. 'We'll all be buzzard bait if Dovel or the Crudups catch us here.'

'Maybe we'd better go in and out of the house through the tunnel,' Yancey suggested. 'Nobody is liable to see us down in the creek bottom. But if we step out of the house up here, anybody on the road from town to a half mile west of here could see us.'

Wade nodded. 'That's right. I'm going out and look for a place close to the end of the tunnel where we can hide the horses.'

Lifting the trap door, he climbed down the ladder. It wasn't hard walking through the tunnel. He didn't have to stoop much until he got near the end. There the tunnel narrowed and lowered until he almost had to crawl to get through.

Once out of the tunnel, he looked up and down the creek bottom. He saw what he was looking for about fifty yards downstream from the tunnel mouth, a small dense grove of cottonwoods. If there was room inside that little grove for three horses, they'd be safe there from prying eyes.

Hurrying down the creek to the place where they had hidden their horses earlier this morning, he untied the animals and led them up to the little grove near the tunnel and tied them. After dark he'd bring feed down from the barn for them and water them at the creek. When he got back to the tunnel mouth, he turned to look at the grove. The horses were completely hidden.

Before going into the tunnel, he remembered the little hole he had seen in the roof. That should be covered. If somebody happened to ride past between the house and the creek, he might see it. That would lead to discovery of the tunnel itself.

Climbing up the little bluff, Wade found a large, flat rock and carried it toward the house, looking for the hole. He found it and laid the rock over it. That would not only hide the hole but protect it as well. From the shape of the hole, he knew that a horse had made it. Apparently Brent Runyan had carved the tunnel a little too near the surface at this place and the thin layer of rock that had been left had not been strong enough to hold up the weight of a horse.

Wade, already halfway to the house from the creek, went on up the gentle slope to the house, after making sure no one was in sight along the road across the creek. Inside the house, he told Prandall and Yancey where he had put the horses, then he and Yancey went into the living room and began some serious planning on how to set up the arrest of the Crudups. In spite of his own conviction that one of the Crudups had killed Brent Runyan, Wade realized he still didn't have any concrete proof to present in court.

'We may have to arrest them for forcing the stage over the bluff,' Yancey said. 'At least you can give eye witness testimony to that.'

'In spite of the masks, I could swear to the identity of Tank, anyway,' Wade said. 'The charge would be murder, too. Four people died.'

Yancey and Wade agreed that to avoid a shoot-out they'd have to wait for an opportunity to get the drop on one of them, preferably Tank, since he would be the easiest one to convict of taking part in wrecking the stage. Once arrested and in jail, Tank might crack and tell the truth about Runyan's death, too.

When they went back into the kitchen to see about finding something to eat, they discovered that Prandall was gone.

'Went out through the tunnel, I reckon,' Yancey said.

'Maybe he's just watching the horses,' Wade said.

The two found that Tank and Tunie had left a well-stocked kitchen. Prandall hadn't come back when dinner was over, and Wade decided to go down into the tunnel and find him.

Wade discovered that the tunnel was darker than before and he realized that the little hole in the roof had let in more light than he had supposed. When he came to the end of the tunnel, he found some limbs moved aside, but Prandall was gone. Wade wondered if Prandall had carelessly left the mouth of the tunnel exposed like this, or if he had departed in a hurry.

Worry lined Wade's forehead. If Prandall had left in a hurry, he must have seen something that called for immediate action. Maybe one of the Crudups had ridden along the road on the other side of the creek. Remembering how determined Prandall was to kill the Crudups, Wade decided that could have been what had happened.

Moving out of the tunnel, Wade replaced the tree limbs over the opening, then hurried down to the grove where he had put the horses. Prandall's horse was missing.

Saddling up, Wade rode down the creek, not even sure this was the way Prandall had gone. But town was in this direction and he reasoned that Prandall might have gone to his store or home for something.

Outside town, he stopped and watched from the water willows along the creek. He saw no sign of Prandall and was about ready to ride back to the tunnel when he saw a wagon coming from the east. He waited, trying to decide who was driving the wagon.

When the wagon stopped in front of the marshal's office and a crowd gathered around it, his curiosity grew. He was sure he recognized Hobie Crudup in the wagon along with Amos Burdeen. It was Burdeen's wagon, he was sure. A saddled horse was tied to the endgate of the wagon.

A premonition of disaster ran over Wade as he saw two men carry something from the wagon into the marshal's office. Was that Prandall? Had he tried to get Hobie and had been killed instead?

Leaving his horse hitched to a large willow,

Wade crossed the creek below the bridge, getting his feet wet, and moved along the back of the buildings facing Main Street. Everyone's attention was concentrated on the marshal's office, so he had little fear of being detected.

At the back of Skarsten's Grocery, he tried the rear door and found it unlocked. Moving into the store, he saw that there were no customers. Cozetta Burdeen was at the front door, looking over at the marshal's office. Effie was nowhere in sight.

Wade moved quietly us the aisle toward the front. 'What's going on out there?' he asked softly.

Cozetta jumped and gasped, wheeling toward him.

'I didn't know anybody else was in the store,' she said. 'Everybody is over at the marshal's office.'

'What did your pa bring in just now?'

'A body,' Cozetta said with a shudder. 'Won't this killing ever stop?'

'Who was killed?'

'Luke Edris. Hobie found him. He had been shot and was propped up against one of the wheels of that wrecked stage.'

Wade was relieved that it wasn't Prandall who was dead. 'Any idea who killed him?'

Cozetta shook her head. 'If they knew you were still in the country, they'd suspect you.'

'Reckon they would, at that,' Wade agreed. 'But I didn't do it. I'd better fade out of the picture, anyway.'

Going out through the rear door, he hurried back across the creek to his horse. He was sure now who had killed Luke Edris. Prandall had included Edris among those who were to be punished for the stage wreck. He wondered if Prandall had been caught.

Riding up the creek, keeping to the lowest ground and in the little willows when he could, he reached the grove of cottonwoods where the horses were hidden. Prandall's horse was there. Tying his horse and unsaddling him, Wade hurried to the tunnel entrance and went inside.

He found Prandall and Yancey in the kitchen, drinking some hot coffee that Yancey had just made.

'We'd better not build any more fires during the daytime,' Wade said. 'The smoke might be seen.' He looked at Prandall. 'Where have you been?'

'Out riding,' Prandall said.

'He wouldn't tell me anything, either,' Yancey said.

'How did you kill Edris?' Wade asked.

Prandall looked up, startled. 'How did you find out about that?'

'I was in town. Cozetta Burdeen told me.'

'She couldn't know I did it,' Prandall said.

'She didn't, but I did. No one else would do it. How did you manage it?'

Prandall smiled. 'I saw him riding toward

town so I got my horse and followed him. He was so surprised to see me, he didn't even put up much of a fight. I took him down to the wrecked stage and propped him up against the wheel. I wanted them to know why he'd been killed—for wrecking that stage.'

'You'll be a marked man if they ever figure it out,' Wade said.

'No worse than I already am,' Prandall said. 'I won't rest until I get both the Crudups, too. I want everybody to know why they died.'

'They might figure you did it; Wade,' Yancey said. 'You were on that stage.'

'Right now, they believe I've left the country. At least, that's what Cozetta thinks.'

'Sure she won't tell them you're still here?' Yancey asked.

Wade nodded. 'I'm sure.'

'What's between you two?' Yancey asked. 'You seem to have an understanding.'

'She took care of me when I was bunged up after the wreck,' Wade said. 'She hated me then because she thought I was Dovel's hired killer. I don't think she's changed her mind too much since she found out different. But I trust her not to tell anybody I'm still in the country.'

'We'd better make our move before anybody else finds out you're still here,' Yancey said.

Wade nodded. 'How about tonight?'

'As soon as it's dark.' Yancey turned to Prandall. 'Can we depend on you to stay here while we're gone?'

Prandall nodded after a moment. 'I reckon I won't have much chance of getting either Tank or Hobie while you two are after them. I'll wait for my chance.'

Wade realized that Yancey was thinking as much of keeping Prandall from killing again as he was of surprising the Crudups himself.

As soon as it was dark, Yancey built a fire in the kitchen stove and they cooked a big supper. Then Yancey and Wade left the house and went down to their horses.

They stayed on the north side of the creek and rode the two and a half miles to the Crudup place. Wade figured that Tank and Tunie had gone back to live with Kate and Hobie. They'd get both Tank and Hobie if they could. But Tank would be the first target if it came to a choice.

Leaving their horses some distance from the house, Wade and Yancey glided quietly up to the house. Yancey moved toward the front door while Wade went around the house to the window where he had climbed in before.

But this time it was different. As Wade went around the corner of the house, he startled a big dog. The dog leaped up, barking furiously. It was the same dog that Tank had with him this morning. Wade was sure he could bluff the dog because he had scared him silly this morning. But that wasn't going to help now. The dog's barking had already done the damage.

Inside the house, a chair scraped against the floor then crashed as it was knocked away. In a minute, bullets would be flying.

CHAPTER THIRTEEN

A door slammed open inside the house as Wade dodged back around the corner. The dog, spurred on by the apparent fear of the intruder, charged after him. Wade wheeled, giving a gruff bark as he had done this morning. The dog stopped so suddenly his feet slid in the dust. Wade made a leap at him and he wheeled back around the corner of the house, yipping as if he'd been kicked.

But Wade had lost valuable time in scaring the dog. Another window popped open on the side of the house where Wade was and a gun roared only a few feet away. The bullet barely missed Wade's head.

Wade dived into the darkness,. But it was Yancey's gun snapping a shot at the window that saved Wade. The gun didn't fire again for a few seconds and when it did, Wade was far enough away so that the darkness had swallowed him.

'Let's ride,' Yancey called and Wade ran toward the sound.

Shots came from the house but they were probing shots now, none coming near their targets. Only when Wade and Yancey mounted and kicked their horses into a run did the bullets start coming in the right direction. But the riders were already out of range.

They had gone a half mile when they reined up to listen. Behind them, they heard the rumble of hoof-beats.

'They're chasing us,' Yancey said. 'We don't want to lead them to our hide-out.'

'You ride north,' Wade said. 'I'll go south. They can't follow us both unless they split up. If they do, I reckon we can handle one apiece.'

Wade reined sharply to the south and splashed across the creek then rode out on the prairie, aiming in the general direction of Jasper Dovel's place. He swung in a wide arc around the buildings, however. After ten minutes, he reined up to listen. There was no sound behind him. He hoped that both the Crudups hadn't followed Yancey, or if they had, that they didn't catch him. More than likely, they had ridden on down the creek, not realizing that Wade and Yancey had left the river.

Reining to the east, Wade went on at an easy lope. It wasn't likely that they would find him now. He didn't turn toward the river until he was almost to town, sure now that he had lost his pursuers. He hoped Yancey had done as well.

He hit the creek and splashed across, reining back to the west toward home.

Suddenly he was aware that there was another rider following him. He reined up, his hand reaching for his gun. Had he completed this circle only to run into the Crudups this near his place?

The rider wasn't trying to be quiet. Wade waited, his gun ready. Only when the horse and rider materialized out of the darkness did his finger relax on the trigger as he recognized Cozetta Burdeen.

'What are you doing up here?' he demanded.

She gasped, jerking her horse to a halt. 'Are you standing guard this far away?' she asked.

'How did you know I was out here?'

'I guessed,' Cozetta said. 'I heard Andy Kent say that this is where you might be holed up if you were still in the country. I also heard Hobie making fun of Tank and Tunie for being afraid of ghosts. I guessed that they had been scared away and I couldn't think of anybody else who would try to scare them off.'

'What are you doing up here?' Wade repeated.

'I was looking for you. After you left town today, Tank rode in. He has decided that it must have been Pa who killed Luke Edris since he was found down close to our place. I'm afraid Tank will kill Pa.'

'How about Hobie?' Wade asked.

'Not Hobie,' Cozetta said. 'He and Pa get along pretty well.'

'Does he still come calling at your place?'

'Once in a while,' Cozetta said defensively. 'Pa thinks it will keep the Crudups friendly toward us.'

'I reckon you can see how friendly they are right now if they're blaming your pa for killing Edris.'

'Pa never hurt anybody.'

'They know that,' Wade said. 'It's just an excuse to run your family out of the valley.'

'Hobie wouldn't have any part in that.'

Anger surged through Wade. 'Hobie is just as mean as Tank.'

'He is not,' Cozetta flashed back. 'I know him better than you do.'

'Hobie is no good,' Wade said. 'Believe me, I know his kind.'

'Why should I believe you?' Cozetta snapped. 'You deceived us once.'

'When?'

'When you made us believe you were Jasper Dovel's hired killer.'

'I didn't say I was. You jumped to that conclusion yourself.'

'You could have told us who you really were.'

'The fewer people who know a secret, the easier it is to keep it,' Wade said.

'You didn't trust us then. Why should I trust you now?'

'No reason at all,' Wade flared angrily. 'Go ahead and buddy up to the Crudups! But don't come crying when they have your pa arrested or killed.'

Wade wheeled his horse around and sent him up the river bank toward the grove where they kept their horses hidden. He heard nothing behind him and wondered if Cozetta had started back home. Wade felt a pang of regret as he rode his horse into the grove and dismounted. Cozetta had come to him with her troubles. Instead of arguing with her, he should have felt complimented. He couldn't deny that he got a warm feeling just thinking that she had sought him out. But he had refused to help her; he had been an idiot.

He was so engrossed with his thoughts that he didn't realize that there was only one other horse in the grove until he had his horse tied. He looked sharply at the horse. It was Yancey's. Prandall's horse was gone. Had the storekeeper sneaked out again? He had caused plenty of trouble the last time he did.

Wade ignored the tunnel entrance. It was dark enough that nobody would see him climbing the bluff. He was almost to the little shed just to the east of the house when an uneasy feeling halted him.

Something or somebody was nearby. He remembered then what Cozetta had said about Andy Kent's guess that Wade might be holed up at the Runyan place if he was still in the country. Had Jasper Dovel figured out that he was here and set a trap for him?

Wade moved forward cautiously. He still hadn't heard any sound he could pinpoint or identify. He was probably just being foolish. But one mistake was more than he was allowed now.

Moving up to the corner of the little shed, he paused, again sampling the feel of the night around him. The uneasiness still persisted.

Suddenly he felt a hard prod in the middle of his back.

'Stand real still,' a voice said. 'Put your hands straight out on either side.'

Wade obeyed slowly, trying to identify that voice. He'd heard it before. It was shrill now, either scared or excited. Then he knew. Cal Fenton. He hadn't heard Maddie's husband speak many times while he had stayed at Dovel's ranch, but that highpitched voice was not easy to forget.

'Jasper must be hard up for a guard to use you,' Wade said slowly.

'I can hold up my end of things,' Fenton said. 'Turn around and put your hands against the wall.'

Wade turned slowly, moving his head so he could see Fenton. The light was poor, but there was no mistaking the fear on Fenton's face. That fear could make him more dangerous than if he were a brave man.

Wade knew his only chance was to outwit or over come Cal Fenton now. Once Fenton got him disarmed and took him to the rest of

Dovel's men, probably in the house, he'd be a dead man. Thinking of the house, he wondered about Ike Yancey. Yancey's horse was in the grove. Dovel's outfit must have captured or killed Yancey already.

As Fenton stepped up to reach for Wade's gun, his own gun sagged a bit in his hand. Wade stuck out a foot and tripped Fenton. Fenton staggered to one side, crashing into the shed. His gun exploded, the bullet angling down into the side of the shed.

Wade wheeled instantly, jerking out his own gun. He prodded it into Fenton's neck so he could feel the cold steel.

'Drop your gun, Fenton. I've got an itchy finger.'

Fenton's gun thudded to the ground. 'It's gone,' he whimpered.

'Where's Yancey?' Wade demanded.

'They're holding him in the house till you come,' Fenton said, breathing hard.

The front door of the house banged open and Maddie's voice cut through the darkness. 'Cal. What did you shoot at?'

'Tell her you just stumbled,' Wade whispered, prodding the gun deeper into Fenton's neck.

Fenton's voice trembled when he spoke. 'I stumbled on a rock.'

Apparently his quivering voice didn't rouse Maddie's suspicions. 'Well, watch where you're going,' she snapped. 'And don't be so scared.

All I'm asking you to do is watch for Tillotson and let me know when he's coming.'

Wade prodded Fenton and he chirped, 'I'll watch, Maddie.'

Wade stood still and didn't allow Fenton to move until he heard the door shut again and everything was quiet in the yard. Then he nudged Fenton over to the shed door.

'How many men did Dovel bring over here?' Wade demanded.

'Mr. Dovel didn't come,' Fenton said. 'Maddie and Andy Kent decided on this. They have just one other man with them. He's out by the barn watching.'

'Where's Kent?'

'In the house holding Yancey.'

Wade slipped the bolt out of the hasp and opened the shed door. He found some rope hanging on the wall where he'd seen it the first day he'd looked in this shed. Tying Fenton's hands behind him and his ankles together, he set him against the inside of the shed. Searching Fenton, he found a big handkerchief in his pocket and made a gag to cover his mouth.

'I'm going to wait out here by this shed until I figure out what to do,' Wade said. 'If you so much as make a sound, bump the wall, or *anything*, I'll come in here and club you to death. Is that clear?'

Fenton mumbled something into the gag. Wade knew he understood. He stepped outside and shut the door and dropped the bolt into place. Turning, he moved silently down the slope to the river. He hoped Fenton would believe he was still standing just outside the door. As long as Fenton thought he was there, he wouldn't make a sound. Wade would bet on that.

*　　　*　　　*

Wade had decided on his next move the minute he conquered Fenton. He lost no time now getting to the mouth of the tunnel. Pushing aside some limbs, he moved inside and hurried along the tunnel to the ladder blocking the end.

Cautiously, he climbed the ladder until his head hit the trap door. Easing up the door, he peered inside the kitchen. There was no light in the house, so Wade couldn't make out anything in the room.

After listening long enough to feel sure there was no one in the kitchen, Wade pushed the trap door up and climbed into the house. Quietly he let the door down then turned to the partition doorway, getting his gun in his hand.

'I hope Tillotson wasn't close enough to hear that shot,' Maddie said finally, breaking the silence and pinpointing her position by the living room window.

'If he did, he'd probably be getting up here

to see what was going on,' Andy Kent said from somewhere near the north wall. 'I wish he'd hurry. This waiting is getting on my nerves,'

'You're not worried about that ghost Tunie saw, are you?' Maddie chided.

'I ain't afraid of no ghost,' Andy said disgustedly. 'But it looks like Tillotson ain't coming back tonight.'

'He'd better,' Maddie said angrily.

'Just what are you going to do about it if he doesn't?'

That was Yancey's voice. But it came from almost exactly the same spot that Wade had marked for Andy Kent. Wade wouldn't dare do anything now. He would have to get Kent first, and he'd be liable to hit Yancey if he tried that.

'You'll be the one who will be sorry if he doesn't come,' Maddie said from the window. 'I'm going to get me a lawman tonight. I'd rather have Tillotson, but I'll take what I can get.'

'Why don't you just shoot me now?' Yancey challenged.

'Don't tempt me,' Maddie said. 'But it's Tillotson I want. If he gets suspicious, I figure he'll try to bargain for your hide. I'll trade you for him any time.'

'He won't bargain,' Yancey said firmly.

Silence fell on the room again. As Wade suspected, Maddie was in command here. Andy Kent would follow her orders. He doubted if Jasper himself could override her decisions if he were here. She was made of the same stuff as Jasper and was thirty years younger.

Wade fingered his gun and tried to think of a way to take advantage of the fact that he was right here in the house with them and they didn't know it. He thought of what Maddie had said about the ghost. She had brought it up. Could she be a little uneasy about that ghost too?

Resurrection of the ghost was the only thing Wade could think of to do except wait. And Maddie was too impatient to wait. Yancey could suffer before Wade got a break.

Using the same weird tone of voice he had used to scare the daylights out of Tunie, he spoke softly, cupping a hand around his mouth. 'Get out of my house.'

For a moment, there was absolute silence in the other room. Then Maddie spoke in a whisper.

'What was that?'

'I don't know,' Andy said. 'Somebody must be in the kitchen.'

'Nobody could get in there without us seeing him,' Maddie said, fear shredding her voice.

'Get out of my house,' Wade repeated, raising his voice a little.

'Somebody's in there, anyway,' Andy said.

Wade stepped back out of the doorway, feeling that Maddie was about to crack. He heard her shuffling around near the window. Suddenly the quiet of the room was shattered by two quick shots through the partition doorway.

Wade spoke again, close to the doorway but out of line from any shots. 'You can't kill me, I'm already dead. Get out of my house.'

Maddie fired three more times, then the hammer of her gun clicked on an empty cylinder.

'Shoot!' Maddie screamed at her foreman. 'Shoot, you fool!'

'What at?' Andy asked. 'I don't see nothing.'

'You hear something, don't you?'

'You can't kill a sound with a bullet,' Andy said.

'Get out of my house,' Wade said louder, in a high pitched voice. 'You can't kill me but I can kill you.'

'I'm going!' Maddie screamed and dashed for the outside door.

Wade turned his attention to the spot where Andy Kent and Yancey were. He heard nothing from there. Then Yancey spoke.

'You'd better do the same, Kent. I've been living here with that ghost. Believe me, I do what he says.'

'Ain't no ghost going to run me out,' Andy said doubtfully.

'Then I won't hold him back any longer,' Yancey said.

Wade heard a crash and guessed that

Yancey had thrown his chair sideways and would be on the floor now. That was his cue. Stepping into the doorway, he fired two quick shots in the direction of the spot where Andy had spoken last.

There was a yell, then boots thundered across the floor. 'I'm going! I'm going!' Andy Kent yelled.

Wade could probably have picked him off by firing at the sound he was making. But he didn't shoot. Kent had all the fight knocked out of him. anyway. Let him think a ghost had shot at him.

Running across to the spot where he had heard the chair crash, Wade found Yancey on the floor, bound to the chair.

'Are you all right?' he asked.

'Will be when you get these ropes off my hands and legs,' Yancey said. He chuckled. 'A ghost sure drains the juices of bravery out of them, doesn't it?'

'They may get those juices back once they get out of the house,' Wade said.

'I'll take my chances against them as soon as I'm untied and get a gun in my hand,' Yancey said.

Wade got the ropes off Yancey's wrists then went to work on his ankles. Outside he heard Maddie screaming for Andy to hurry. But Andy was yelling that they had to get Fenton out of the shed. Evidently Fenton had banged against the shed wall enough to get their attention. Another voice joined in, asking what was going on. That would be the man Maddie had stationed at the barn. Maddie screamed an answer but she was farther away now, apparently moving fast.

Finally it was quiet outside. Yancey was free and had located his gun where it had been tossed into a corner.

'They know we're living here now,' Yancey said. 'We can't hide any longer.'

'Where's Prandall? His horse is gone again.'

'He was gone when I got here,' Yancey said. 'Maybe Maddie found him or ran him off. They were waiting for me. It was dark so I came up the hill. Walked right into the business end of a gun. I thought they'd kill me, but they decided instead to use me for bait to catch you.'

'Almost got us both,' Wade said. 'We'll have to strike fast now if we're going to catch the Crudups by surprise.'

CHAPTER FOURTEEN

Wade was worried about George Prandall. He would have been glad to know that Maddie had just. scared him off, but he doubted that. Knowing that he had tried to kill Jasper Dovel, she would more than likely kill him if she got the chance.

'His horse was gone,' Wade said, reassuring himself. 'If Maddie had killed him, his horse would still be there, wouldn't it? I'll watch the first half of the night to make sure Dovel's outfit doesn't come back and see if George does.'

'I'll take the last half,' Yancey agreed.

Morning found nothing changed. Yancy had breakfast ready by the time Wade came into the kitchen shortly after dawn.

'Figured we'd better get on the prowl early to see if we can find George,' Yancey said.

'After we find him, we'll arrest Tank and maybe Hobie.'

Yancey sighed. 'That sounds easy, but it won't be.'

'Don't figure it will be,' Wade said.

As soon as they had eaten, they climbed down into the tunnel. There was the chance that the Crudups had not discovered that Wade and Yancey were still around. Wade had the feeling that the Dovels and the Crudups were in two separate camps now, with little or no communication between them. Kate Crudup was driving hard for domination of this valley.

'Let's head toward town,' Yancey suggested. 'He might have gone home for something.'

They found him before they got to town. The sun was up when Wade saw something off to the south of the willows that caused him to rein his horse in that direction.

George Prandall was lying just the way he had fallen from his horse. There was no sign of the horse.

'Shot square in the middle,' Yancey said, kneeling beside the storekeeper.

'Wonder who did it,' Wade said. 'Could have been one of the Crudups. Or it could have been one of Maddie's crew last night.'

'What would Maddie's bunch be doing down here?'

'I saw Cozetta Burdeen out here last night,' Wade said. 'She told me that Andy Kent was in town yesterday guessing that maybe I was holed up in Runyan's place. Maddie might have been there, too.

They could have met George as they were coming out to pay us that visit.'

'What was Cozetta doing out at night?'

Wade signed. 'Looking for some help, I reckon, and I didn't give her any. Tank Crudup is accusing her pa of killing Luke Edris. I figure he's trumped that up just to scare Amos Burdeen out of the valley. I should have told Cozetta that George Prandall killed Edris, but I didn't.'

'It probably wouldn't have stopped the Crudups from running Burdeen out, anyway,'

'You're right,' Wade agreed. 'What are we going to do about George? We can't just ride in with the body. That will announce to the whole valley that we're still here.'

'I'll slip a note into the marshal's office that

there's a dead man out here. Let Deuce take it from there.'

'Be careful,' Wade warned. 'Deuce is Dovel's man. After last night, you're likely a marked man too, because you can testify that they were planning to bushwhack me.'

'Wait for me at the bridge,' Yancey said. 'I'll only be a couple of minutes.'

True to his word, Yancey had been gone from the river only a few minutes when he returned. Wade turned up the creek again with Yancey beside him.

'Straight to Crudups'?' Yancey asked.

Wade nodded. But a short distance from the Runyan place, he held up his hand, stopping the horses in the water willows. Wade pointed to three riders moving up the slope to the house.

'Looks like we won't have to go to the Crudups' place,' he said. 'That's Tank and Hobie and Kate right there.'

'Yeah,' Yancey said. 'And they're going to the house. Probably Kate is going to convince Tank there are no ghosts in that house.'

'Let's go up the tunnel,' Wade said.

Leaving their horses in the cottonwood grove, Wade and Yancey hurried to the tunnel mouth and went inside, rearranging the branches over the opening behind them. Under the trap door, they stopped.

'They're up there,' Wade whispered.

'Let's find out what they're doing so we can

surprise them,' Yancey suggested.

Kate's voice was shrill and cut through the stillness of the house like a knife. 'If you're too big a coward to stay here, Tank, we'll put Hobie here. Jasper knows now we're putting the bind on him. No telling what he might do. We've got to have somebody live between Jasper and town to keep tabs on what he's doing so he can't pull a fast one on us.'

'I ain't scared,' Tank said, but his voice wasn't convincing. 'I just don't want to stay anywhere without Tunie. And wild horses couldn't pull her back here. We've already got most of Uncle Jasper's cattle. He ain't got a leg to stand on right now, if he just knew it.'

'We've got his money and we'll soon have his valley,' Hobie said with a laugh.

'We'll have to get rid of the Burdeens,' Kate said. 'I know you're sweet on that Burdeen girl, Hobie, but we can't let that squatter stay in this country, knowing what he knows about that stage wreck.'

'No skin off my nose, Ma,' Hobie said. 'Cozetta has been acting as cool as a water jug lately, anyway.'

'Trumping up that murder charge against Amos Burdeen ought to send him skitting,' Kate said. 'I wonder who did kill Luke.'

'I figure it was Prandall,' Tank said. 'He swore he'd get every one who helped wreck that stagecoach. He knew who did it, all right. That's why I killed him last night when I got the chance. He wasn't no fighter, but he could shoot you in the back as well as anybody.'

'I'm glad you got him,' Kate said. 'Now we'll put the pressure on Burdeen till he hightails it. Then we'll tell Jasper which foot the shoe is on and we'll take over. If there's anybody in town who don't like it, he can get out or stay permanently in the stone orchard.'

'I'll stay here at the house part of the time, Ma,' Hobie promised. 'Enough to make sure Uncle Jasper doesn't try something.'

'Tank, you head down to Burdeens' and put the pressure on Amos. Give him till tomorrow noon to decide what he's going to do.'

'All right, Ma,' Tank said. 'Better come with me, Hobie. At least he won't shoot me till I get down to the house if you're along.'

The three left the house quickly. Wade pushed up the trap door and crawled into the kitchen, Yancey right behind him.

'Would you look at that?' Yancey said, running to the living room window. 'They're riding off already. They sure don't waste time once they decide to do something.'

'We haven't got a chance of catching them, either. Our horses are down in the grove. If we barge out there and try to arrest them now, they'll either getaway or pen us up here in the house and burn it down.'

'We've got to get a better chance than this,' Yancey agreed. 'Let's ride down the creek and spring an ambush on Tank and Hobie when they come back from Burdeens'. Didn't sound like Kate was going to go with them.'

Wade agreed and they went back into the tunnel and hurried out to the creek. Getting their horses, they rode down stream. Wade studied the tracks. He saw where Kate had cut off to go back toward her home. A little farther, the other two horses had crossed the creek.

'They're going down to Burdeens' on the road south of the creek,' Wade said. 'They'll probably come back the same way. How about surprising them right here?'

'Perfect,' Yancey agreed. 'You hide here in the willows. I'll go back and hide behind that bluff. We can cover them from two angles that way.'

Wade dismounted and Yancey took both horses back into the bluffs out of sight. Wade nestled down into as comfortable a position as he could. He had been settled no more than ten minutes, expecting at least an hour's wait, when a voice directly behind startled him.

'Don't move, Tillotson. If you do, it will be your last.'

Wade slowly turned his head to look at Deuce Ulrich. The marshal must have seen him stop here in these willows. He was only a short distance from town.

'What do you figure on doing?' Wade asked.

'I'm taking you over to Jasper Dovel. He'll be pleased to see you.'

'Probably will be,' Wade admitted. 'What's in it for you?'

'Mr. Dovel put a big reward on your head,' Deuce said. 'I figure I might as well get it as anybody.'

'I suppose that is your privilege,' Wade said. He saw Yancey leave his hiding place behind the bluff and move silently up behind Deuce but he gave no indication to Deuce that he wasn't helpless. 'Just how do you figure on getting me to Dovel's ranch?'

'I'll make you walk,' Deuce said. 'I'll ride along and shoot you down if you try to get away.'

'I wouldn't be so sure of that,' Yancey said from ten feet behind Deuce. 'Just drop your gun, marshal. You've got no cause to arrest Wade.'

Deuce's face turned a sickly green and the gun slipped from his fingers. He turned to look at Yancey. 'I saw you leave. What made you come back?'

'I wanted to see your pretty face again,' Yancey said sarcastically.

'You're a sheriff,' Deuce exploded. 'You're interfering with the law.'

'Wade is a deputy U.S. marshal. Looked to me like you were interfering with him. Tell you what. I'll give you a chance to arrest Wade on even terms. Put your gun back where it belongs, then draw against him.'

'Now hold on,' Deuce said. 'I don't want to

kill him. That's up to Mr. Dovel.'

'Maybe you won't have to kill him. See that rock just across the creek? Draw and shoot at that. Maybe you're fast enough to scare Wade so much he won't want to draw against you. If so, you can take him without a fight.'

Deuce grinned. He picked up his gun and dropped it in his holster. With a fast slap, he brought it up and fired. He missed the rock but not by too many inches.

'Good enough,' Yancey said. 'Now put your gun away again. Wade, it's your turn.'

Wade made his fastest draw and his first shot spurted sand over the rock. Deuce's eyes widened. He apparently considered himself fast with a gun, but he couldn't help knowing he was slow in comparison to Wade.

'Now then,' Yancey said, 'if Wade isn't too scared, you two back off about twenty paces and have at it.'

'Hold on,' Deuce sputtered. 'I told you I didn't want to kill him, just take him to Mr. Dovel.'

'The only way you're going to do that is to outdraw him,' Yancey said. 'I'll put my gun away and I won't interfere.'

Deuce sputtered some more and began backing toward the willows where he had left his horse. 'I'll let Mr. Dovel come after him himself.'

'You'd better make sure you do let somebody else do it,' Yancey said, none of the humor in his voice now.

'I won't bother him or you any more,' Deuce said.

He got his horse and spurred him back toward town. Wade watched him go, grinning at Yancey.

'You sort of took the wind out of his sails, Ike.'

'Better than killing him,' Yancey said. 'He thought he was fast.'

'I doubt if our ambush will work after all that shooting,' Wade said.

'Tank and Hobie should be done at Burdeens' now,' Yancey said. 'Maybe they didn't hear the shooting. Let's stick around and see.'

Wade agreed and they settled back into their original hiding places. Time dragged on until Wade was sure that more than an hour had passed. Still they waited. Wade wondered if the Crudups had gone home a different way.

After another quarter of an hour, Wade was ready to call Yancey and suggest they give up. Then he saw a rider coming from town. Before the rider had come far, he recognized Fanny Ulrich. She was heading almost straight for his hiding place.

Wade stood up. There wasn't going to be any ambush, anyway. Fanny, seeing him, spurred straight toward him, splashing across the creek. He saw the alarm in her face.

'What's wrong?' he demanded.

'Several things,' Fanny said, sliding off her horse. 'Pa told me what happened out here. You could have killed him.'

'Maybe,' Wade said. 'But there was no point in that. You didn't ride down here to tell me that, did you?'

'No,' Fanny admitted, watching Yancey come down from his hiding place behind the bluff. 'I came to tell you Cozetta's in trouble. You haven't fooled me any, Wade, even if you have fooled her. I know she means a lot to you, so I wanted to give you a chance to help her. I owe you that for sparing Pa.'

'Hold up a second,' Wade said. 'What kind of trouble is Cozetta in?'

'Mr. Burdeen just walked into town. Tank and Hobie were down there threatening him for murdering Luke Edris. They said they'd let him off if he'd move out. When he refused, Hobie took Cozetta and said he'd keep her until Mr. Burdeen agreed to leave.'

CHAPTER FIFTEEN

'You mean Hobie kidnapped Cozetta?' Wade demanded.

Fanny nodded. 'That's how I understood it. Mr. Burdeen is so upset, it's hard to say exactly what did happen.'

Yancey reached them then. 'Who was

kidnapped?' he asked.

'Cozetta,' Wade said. 'Hobie Crudup took her.'

'That's just dandy!' Yancey exploded. 'No wonder they didn't come back this way.'

'Where did he take her?' Wade asked Fanny.

'I don't know,' Fanny said. 'I suppose Mr. Burdeen may know. I'm afraid if he goes after her, he may blunder around and get himself and her both killed.'

'Could be,' Wade agreed. 'Where is Amos now?'

'He's in Pa's office. I don't know how long he'll stay there. He's half crazy.'

'I want to talk with him,' Yancey said.

Wade shook his head. 'I'd better do this alone.'

'Just what have you got in mind?'

'I'm not sure till I talk to Amos,' Wade said. 'I imagine Hobie left word with Amos where to get in touch with him.'

'And you're figuring on taking his place?' Yancey guessed.

'Maybe,' Wade said. 'I'll see what the situation is. If I do go instead of Amos, I'll have to go alone. If two of us came after her, Hobie might kill Cozetta. I wouldn't put anything past him.'

Yancey considered it for a moment. 'All right. I guess maybe Cozetta is your problem, not mine. You take care of it your way.'

'She's Amos's problem right now,' Wade

said. 'But I don't think he can handle it.'

Wade turned and ran to his horse. He had wasted too much time already.

'I'll keep things under control at home,' Yancey called as Wade headed toward town, Fanny beside him.

Wade's mind was seething as he rode the short distance to town. Fanny was still with him as he thundered down the main street and pulled his horse to a stop in front of the marshal's office. Effie Skarsten was standing in the doorway of her store next to Ulrich's office.

'Are you going after Cozetta?' she asked Wade.

'I'm going to talk to Amos,' Wade said. 'Got to find out what Hobie has done and what orders he left for Amos to follow. Have you talked to him?'

'Tried to. He doesn't make much sense.'

Wade hurried into the marshal's office. Deuce was standing in front of Amos Burdeen, who was hunched down in a chair in front of the cold stove.

'What happened, Amos?' Wade demanded.

Amos Burdeen looked up at Wade and if ever Wade had seen a tortured soul rejected in a man's face, he saw it then.

'Hobie and Tank came down,' Amos said almost in a whisper. 'Told me I was going to be arrested and hanged for murdering Luke Edris. I told them I hadn't even seen Edris in a week. That didn't make any difference. Then they said if I'd leave the country, they'd see to it I'd go free.'

'Did they offer to buy your place?'

Amos shook his head. 'Just told me move out. I've worked for three years building that place up. It's all me and Ruth and Cozetta have. I told them I wouldn't give it up.'

A sob shook the homesteader and the words choked in his throat.

'Is that when they took Cozetta?' Wade asked.

Amos nodded. 'Cozetta didn't come in to work at Effie's today. Effie said she could get along without her, so she stayed home to help Ruth make a dress. I bought the goods for Ruth a month ago.'

'Where did Hobie take her?' Wade demanded. 'What did he tell you to do?'

Amos looked up at Wade again. 'He said he was taking her to Peterson's old place. If I changed my mind about moving out, I was to come there and tell him and he'd let Cozetta go.'

Wade looked at Deuce. 'Where's the Peterson place?'

'About half a mile south of the creek and another mile east of Burdeen's,' Deuce said. 'Peterson moved out over a year ago.'

'Run out by Jasper Dovel,' Effie said from the doorway. 'The house and barn are still there.'

'What do you figure on doing?' Wade asked Burdeen.

'I'm going to leave the country,' Amos said as if the decision had been hard to make, but was a relief now that he had reached it.

'Why didn't you tell him that then?'

Amos shook his head. 'I thought at first I just couldn't leave. But I can—to save Cozetta. I want to get her out of his hands.'

'I thought it was your idea that Cozetta keep company with Hobie,' Wade said, wishing almost instantly that he hadn't said it. Amos Burdeen didn't need condemnation now.

'Hobie acted halfway civilized,' Amos said, face twisted in agony. 'I thought we could stay here if we kept peace with the Crudups. Now I wish I had shot him the first time he set foot on the place!'

'Did Hobie give you any special instructions about getting Cozetta back?' Wade demanded.

Amos shook his head. 'I just have to ride over to Peterson's and tell him I'm pulling out. At least, that's all he said.'

Wade shot a glance at Deuce and Effie. Effie shook her head.

'I wouldn't depend on that,' she said. 'Hobie is Satan without the tail. I figure he aims to get Amos over there and then kill him. He might even kill Cozetta, too. He's capable of it.'

Wade looked at Deuce. 'Keep Amos here. Is there any way I can get to the Peterson place without being seen?'

'You're going after Cozetta?' Effie asked with satisfaction.

'I figure I've got a better chance against Hobie than Amos would have,' Wade said. 'Anyway, I've got a score to settle with Hobie.'

'If you want to sneak in on the Peterson place,' Deuce said, 'ride south of town for half a mile then turn east. You'll come to a wash that runs right behind the barn. But don't underestimate Hobie. He's tricky and he'll be watching for Amos.'

Wade nodded, thinking how much Deuce had changed since they had met a couple of hours ago out by the creek. Then he realized that Deuce was Jasper Dovel's man. The way things stood now, any man supporting Dovel would be glad to see trouble come to one of the Crudups.

As Wade started toward the door, Amos got up to follow. Deuce took him by the shoulder and set him back down.

'Let him handle it,' Deuce said. 'He's a marshal. He knows how to do things like this.'

Wade mounted his horse and rode south down Main Street and was out of town and on the unbroken prairie in less than a block. Remembering Deuce's instructions, he rode an estimated half mile then reined due east. He covered a couple of miles without seeing anything. Then, as he topped a rise, he spotted some buildings about half a mile ahead.

Reining up quickly, he stood on his toes in the stirrups and studied the buildings, just his head in view of anyone watching from the buildings. Evidently the wash Deuce had mentioned was ahead. He'd have to ride over this knoll to get to it. Anyone watching from the homestead could see him.

After a moment's deliberation, Wade dismounted and ground reined his horse. Advancing on foot, he reached the top of the rise. From ground level, the buildings were barely visible. Moving slowly and well stooped over, he crossed the high ground and dropped down into the wash. He wished he had his horse then. The wash was deep enough that he could ride here without being in sight of the buildings.

As the wash led down behind the barn, however, it shallowed out until a rider would have been clearly visible. Crouching as he ran, Wade kept out of sight of the house. If Hobie was in the barn, he'd see Wade, but that was a chance he would just have to take.

He wondered if Hobie would have killed Amos if he had offered a complete surrender to Hobie's terms. Wade suspected that he would have. Hobie and Tank were different in manner, but basically they were the same—killers. If Hobie had killed Amos, he surely would have killed Cozetta too. There would have been no witness then to Amos's murder, only suspicion. And suspicion was too weak a rope to hang a man.

At the corner of the barn he paused to catch his breath. Moving to a window that had once had a sack for a covering, he peered through the shreds of the sack into the interior. It was too dark to see much. A door and another small window were on the opposite side, facing the house.

Finding a rear door hanging half off its hinges, Wade slipped inside the barn without moving the door. Standing still until his eyes grew accustomed to the dimness, he searched the barn. Peterson had left very little when he pulled out. A broken fork and some leather straps were all Wade saw.

He moved to the front of the barn and looked at the house. Nothing stirred there, either, and he wondered if Amos had been confused about where Hobie had taken Cozetta. Or maybe Hobie hadn't taken her where he said he would.

The yard between the house and barn was grown over with weeds, but there was no cover out there for a man. If he left the barn and tried to cross the yard, anybody in the house could pick him off like shooting a can off a post.

Wade tried to remember exactly how Amos Burdeen talked. Could he imitate Amos's voice well enough to fool Hobie? He might, since Hobie would be expecting Amos.

Wade yelled in a voice he hoped would

sound something like Amos. 'Hobie?'

For a long minute there was nothing but silence, then Hobie yelled back from the house. 'That you, Amos?'

'Yeah,' Wade yelled. 'We're leaving the country. Turn Cozetta loose.'

'Step out where I can see you,' Hobie yelled.

Wade realized that his imitation of Amos Burdeen probably hadn't been good enough. 'I ain't fixing to get shot,' he called back.

'I won't shoot you,' Hobie called. 'Come on over and get Cozetta.'

Wade wasn't sure whether Hobie hadn't been fooled by Wade's imitation of Amos's voice, or whether he just wanted to get Amos out where he could kill him.

'I ain't showing myself,' Wade shouted back. 'Send Coezetta out and we'll leave the country. That's what you wanted.'

'I want to see you first,' Hobie yelled. It was a stalemate. Wade had no intention of showing himself, and apparently Hobie had no intention of giving up Cozetta without getting his shot at the man in the barn, whether he thought it was Amos Burdeen or somebody else.

Wade moved over to a place where the cracks between the boards were spreading with age. Through the cracks he could see the house with no risk of being seen himself. He couldn't see any movement, but he knew

Hobie was there.

He fixed his eyes on the front of the house and almost missed the movement at the far corner. Hobie had slipped around the house, apparently going out a rear door or window. Now he dashed silently across the yard, out of view from the front of the barn.

Wade moved quickly to the north side of the barn and tried to locate Hobie through the cracks. He couldn't do it, but he guessed that Hobie planned to go around the barn and try to shoot him in the back from the rear window.

He heard a crash over at the house. He guess that Hobie had left Cozetta tied up and she was trying to get free. Maybe she had fallen against something. But he had no time to think about that now. He must locate Hobie.

He listened carefully for any movement outside the barn, but he heard nothing. Then Cozetta screamed from the house.

'Pa, he's coming to the barn to kill you!'

As if that was a signal, Hobie plunged through the rear doorway of the barn, the way Wade had come in. Hobie apparently thought he had reached the barn unnoticed until Cozetta's scream had given him away. He was trying to strike while surprise was still a valuable ally.

Wade, however, was only mildly astonished to find that Hobie had gotten all the way around to the rear door. Hobie hit the floor of the barn and rolled. Wade waited patiently. Not only would Hobie's eyes be unaccustomed to the dingy interior of the barn, but he'd also be disoriented by his roll.

When Hobie came up on one knee, searching for the man in the barn, Wade had his gun on Hobie.

'Drop that gun, Hobie!' Wade snapped.

Hobie wheeled toward the sound, his gun roaring. The bullet missed Wade by no more than an inch. While he had hesitated to shoot a man who hadn't even seen him yet, Wade didn't hesitate to shoot a man who was trying to kill him.

His shot was quick and, though Hobie was throwing himself sideways, the bullet did not miss. Hobie fired once more and so did Wade. Hobie missed again but both of Wade's bullets hit home.

Wade checked to make sure that Hobie wouldn't be shooting anymore, then he went to the front door.

'Are you alone over there, Cozetta?' he yelled, thinking that Tank could very well be with Cozetta now.

'Yes,' she shouted back. 'It that you, Pa?'

'No, it's Wade Tillotson.'

Wade dashed across the yard, still unsure of the situation. Tank could have come out here with Hobie. But nothing stopped him as he sprinted across to the door of the house and burst inside.

Cozetta was lying on the floor, still tied to a three-legged chair that the Petersons apparently hadn't felt was worth hauling away with them. It had been that unbalanced chair that had upset with Cozetta.

Quickly Wade untied Cozetta. 'Are you all right?' he asked.

he nodded. 'All except for a sore arm where I fell. What happened out there?'

Hobie came in shooting,' Wade said and let it drop at that.

He looked at Cozetta. Her hair was rumpled and out of place. Some of the fear that had gripped her still lingered in her face. Yet she was as beautiful in his eyes as she had ever been. Maybe it was just reaction to his relief at getting her free from Hobie. That hour that he'd known she was Hobie's prisoner had made him realize how important she was to him.

He reached for her and without a sound she came to him as if it was the most natural thing in the world to do. At that moment, Wade felt that it was.

Wade found two horses where Hobie had hidden them in a draw east of the house. Apparently Hobie had expected Amos to sneak into the barn and he didn't want him to know for sure that Hobie was in the house. He would have known if he'd found the horses there.

Riding Hobie's horse, Wade led the way back to pick up his own horse. Then they turned north to Burdeen's place. Cozetta stayed with her mother while Wade rode on to town and reported to Deuce and Amos what happened. Deuce said he'd send someone out to bring in Hobie's body.

'I don't know how to thank you,' Amos Burdeen said, pumping Wade's hand. 'I reckon I could have done that.'

'I figure you could have if you'd had to,' Wade said. knowing he was stretching the truth but feeling it was worth it to restore some of Amos's confidence. 'Take care of your family now. Yancey and I have to bring in Tank.'

Wade rode home, not bothering to go up the tunnel this time. Everybody knew where he was staying now. He didn't see Yancey's horse, but he supposed that Yancey had left him in the grove. There were tracks in the yard, likely left by Maddie's crew last night.

As he stepped inside the house, a groan greeted him and his hand dropped to his gun. He started cautiously across the living room, wondering if this could be another trap.

Then he saw Ike Yancey lying on the floor just inside the kitchen, blood soaking the front of his shirt.

CHAPTER SIXTEEN

Dropping on one knee beside Yancey, Wade quickly examined him. He'd been shot in the chest. The bullet apparently hadn't hit any vital organ or Yancey would have been dead. He had bled a lot.

'Who shot you?' Wade asked.

Yancey opened his eyes. 'Tank. He was in the house when I came in. Surprised me. Left me for dead.'

'I'll get a wagon and take you into town,' Wade said. 'You'll get good care there.'

Wade rode back to town at a gallop. Remembering the horse doctor Jasper Dovel had sent him for when his family had gotten sick on the cornmeal, he stopped at the house on the west edge of town. The old man was there and agreed to go out with him to see the wounded man. Wade rode on to the livery barn and got the boy there to hitch up a team and wagon. The doctor rode with Wade in the wagon as they left town.

Wade was afraid he'd find Yancey dead when he got back, but Yancey seemed no worse than when he'd left. The doctor made a quick examination, then announced that the bullet had gone all the way through without hitting anything vital. He gave Yancey some laudanum to ease the pain before they moved him.

Fanny had seen Wade leaving town with the livery wagon and was coming to find out what had happened. She met the wagon half way to town. At her insistance, they took Yancey to Deuce Ulrich's and there Fanny made him a bed on a cot in Deuce's room.

'We have to make sure that Tank doesn't find out that Yancey is still alive,' Wade said.

'Nobody will find out where he is if you can keep the doc from telling,' Fanny promised.

Wade warned the old man not to say a word or he'd answer to him. The doctor promised. Then, assured that Yancey was going to make it all right, he went back to the wagon.

Wade drove the doctor home, then took the wagon back to the livery barn where he had left his horse. As he was leading his horse out of the barn, he saw Cozetta hurrying down the street from the main part of town.

'I've been looking for you,' Cozetta panted as she reached him. 'Mr. Ulrich said you were in town. Maddie Fenton is out to get you. She's got two of her father's hands with her.'

'That's not so surprising,' Wade said. 'How did you find it out?'

'We had to have some groceries. I started after them and met Pa coming home. He came back with me; wouldn't let me come alone. We were in Effie's store when Maddie came in to inquire about you.'

'Your pa is right in not letting you run around alone. Where is he now?'

'He went over to see Mr. Ulrich. I don't think the marshal will be any help.'

'I doubt it myself. Thanks for the warning.' He mounted and reined his horse down the street.

'Where are you going?' Cozetta asked in alarm.

'To find Maddie,' Wade said. 'I'm tired of running away from trouble. The quickest way to get rid of it is to hunt it down.'

'Oh!' Cozetta said in exasperation. 'I shouldn't have told you anything. Then at least you'd have gotten out of town.'

'Maybe and maybe not, if Maddie saw me. You say she's in Effie's store?'

Cozetta nodded. 'She was there with Andy Kent and another one of Dovel's men. Don't go in there.'

Wade ignored her and rode down to the front of the vacant building north of Skarsten's Grocery and dismounted. Cozetta was beside him when he started over to the store.

'You stay here,' Wade ordered.

'I will not,' Cozetta said. 'You wouldn't even have known Maddie was in town if I hadn't told you. What are you going to do if Maddie starts shooting?'

'Don't rightly know,' Wade admitted. 'But when somebody is shooting at you, it's hard to distinguish between a man and a woman. The bullets all feel the same.'

At the corner of the store, Wade hesitated

then dodged forward and slammed through the door, his gun in his hand. The store was empty except for Effie.

'What is this, a hold up?' Effie demanded.

'I heard Maddie Fenton was here looking for me.'

'She was,' Effie said calmly. 'Looking for you and Ike Yancey. She had a couple of men with her, too. They went out to look through the town while Maddie stayed here.'

'Where is she now?' Wade demanded.

'Come here and I'll show you,' Effie said smugly.

Wade followed Effie toward the back of the store. Cozetta was just a step behind. Effie opened the door into a little storeroom. Maddie Fenton was sitting against a barrel of flour, her hands and ankles tied and a gag in her mouth.

'Why did you tie her up?' Wade asked.

'I didn't figure you needed a hellcat like her chasing you while you were watching for Tank. You killed Hobie and you can be sure that Tank will be gunning for you. So I tied her up and put her back here where no one will find her unless I want them to.'

Wade nodded. 'You're right, I don't need her gunning for me, too. I'd like to ask her some questions, though. Take the gag out of her mouth.'

'I wouldn't believe a word she says,' Effie said. But she stooped and pulled the rag out of her mouth.

'Where's Jasper?' Wade asked.

Maddie spit angrily as though the rag in her mouth had left a bad taste. Then for a full minute she swore steadily at Effie and Wade. Finally Wade cut her off by repeating the question sharply.

'He's gone to get Aunt Kate,' Maddie snapped. 'He'll kill her if he finds her.'

'Has he finally figured out she's undercutting him?' Wade asked.

'He knows Aunt Kate and Tank and Hobie have been stealing us blind. It was the biggest mistake he ever made bringing them here.'

Wade nodded. 'Why weren't you out after the Crudups, too? Why were you looking for me and Yancey?'

Maddie spit again. 'Why do you think? Pa finally came to his senses and decided to clean out the whole valley. That means his own sister, Tank and Hobie, and you two star toters as well as the nesters. I came to get you while he went after the Crudups. Just because I'm tied up right now, don't think you're going to get away. I've got men looking for you. You'll never get out of town.'

'You were right, Effie,' Wade said. 'She does look better tied up and gagged. Can't say that I enjoy hearing her talk.'

Effie reached down and jammed the rag back in Maddie's mouth, almost getting bitten in the process. With the gag fastened securely in place, they backed out of the storeroom and Effie slammed the door.

'She is a spitfire,' Wade said. 'What about these men she's got roaming around town looking for me?'

'Watch out for them,' Effie said. 'Until they find out that Maddie isn't giving the orders now, they're dangerous. Without either Maddie or Jasper to run things, the rest of Jasper's crew wouldn't hurt anybody.'

'You'd better stay here in the store,' Cozetta said. 'They'll soon come back here for more orders from Maddie. You can surprise them.'

Wade nodded. 'I thought of that. But I can't wait. Jasper and the rest of his men may decide to burn my place. If he is set on cleaning out the valley, he'll burn every homestead along the creek if he's not stopped.'

'So you're going to risk your neck to protect your place,' Effie said disgustedly. 'You'd better protect your hide. That's more important.'

'I'll take care of that, too,' Wade said and went out the door.

Before he reached his horse in front of the vacant building, he realized that Cozetta had mounted her horse in front of the store and was following him.

Wade mounted, then turned to Cozetta. 'Where do you think you're going?'

'With you,' Cozetta said. 'I can shoot if I have to. And Pa and Ma can't stay here, either, if Jasper Dovel is determined to clean all the homesteaders out of the valley.'

'I could run into bad trouble,' Wade said. 'I don't want you getting hurt.'

'I could get hurt right here in town, too. I'm going with you.'

Wade realized she had more determination than he had thought. At that, she might be safer with him at his house than she would be here in town with Maddie's men running loose.

'Better tell your pa where you're going. He's had enough scares for one day.'

'All right,' Cozetta agreed. 'But you wait for me.'

Wade didn't have any choice. If she was going with him, he wanted her close to him all the time. Maddie had made it clear that Jasper had declared open season on all lawmen and homesteaders, so Cozetta wasn't safe, either.

Cozetta didn't even dismount in front of the marshal's office, but called in to her father that she was going with Wade. Before he could object, she reined her horse around and rode back to Wade.

They turned down the street and rode at a gallop straight to the creek and across the bridge. It was the quickest way out of town and Wade didn't want to collide with the two men Maddie had searching the town for him.

At the homestead, Wade decided to hide the horses in the grove. If the horses were up by the house, it would announce to anyone passing by that Wade was there. With Cozetta along, he especially wanted to avoid a battle. Let the Crudups and Dovels have it out among themselves.

Leaving the horses in the cottonwoods, Wade led Cozetta to the tunnel and they went into the house through the trap door. Once in the house, Wade hurried to the window to look out. He had a good view in both directions along the creek. He spotted a rider almost instantly to the southwest.

'Does that look to you like either Tank Crudup or Jasper Dovel?' he asked.

Cozetta looked hard at the figure. The rider was half a mile away.

'It's not Tank,' Cozetta said finally. 'Doesn't look like a big man. Jasper Dovel is big, too. Maybe it's Kate.'

Wade nodded. 'Could be. Whoever it is seems to be coming here.' He watched the rider come closer until he could positively identify Kate Crudup. 'She's probably coming to make certain Yancey is dead. She knows some things I'd sure like to find out.'

'Nobody could get her to tell any secrets,' Cozetta said.

'I'm not so sure about that,' Wade said thoughtfully. He hurried to the other room and got the broom out of the pantry where he had put it after scaring Tank and Tunie. 'Get a sheet off the bed. This ghost scared Tunie. And I think Kate's afraid of ghosts, too, from what I heard her say.'

'That doesn't look like a ghost to me,' Cozetta said. But she went into the bedroom and brought back a sheet.

The cross piece was still nailed to the broom handle. It took Wade only a minute to get the sheet in place and the broom hung again on the wires. Then he and Cozetta got down into the tunnel and Wade stopped two steps up the ladder with the trap door slightly open.

He didn't have much time to spare. Kate came into the house cautiously, apparently not sure who might be here. Assured there was nothing moving in sight, she came on to the kitchen where she spotted the blood where Yancey had lain.

She still hadn't seen the ghost hanging from the wire up in the corner of the kitchen. Wade gave the string some slack and the broom started sliding slowly down the wires toward the partition door.

'Why did you come back?' Wade intoned.

Kate gasped and, looking up, saw the sheet moving down toward her. She screamed and wheeled to run.

'Don't run or I'll kill you,' Wade said.

Kate stopped, almost with one foot in the air. 'Wh-what do you want?'

'Why did you kill me?'

'I didn't kill you, Yancey,' Kate wailed. 'Tank did.'

'I'm not Ike Yancey,' Wade intoned. 'I'm the ghost of Brent Runyan.'

'I—I—I killed you because my boys bungled the job,' Kate stuttered.

It was Wade's turn to be shocked. He had hoped to scare Kate into telling which of her sons had killed Brent. He hadn't expected her to confess doing it herself.

Wade wasn't sure what to do now. Then a horse galloped into the yard and boots thumped outside. Kate seemed to come out of her paralysis. She screamed again and started running toward the door. She had just reached it when Tank met her.

'Where are you going, Ma?' he demanded.

'There's a ghost in there! Brent Runyan's ghost!' She tried to get past him but his bulk filled the doorway.

'There ain't no such thing as a ghost, Ma. That's what you told me yourself. I've been doing some thinking and you're right. There's a trick to it.' He took Kate by the arm and dragged her hack into the house.

Wade saw that Tank was going to come right into the kitchen in spite of the ghost. It was broad daylight now and anyone who really looked could see what the ghost was made of. Tank was going to look.

Wade lowered the trap door and stepped off the ladder, motioning Cozetta down the tunnel away from the door. He heard Tank tramping across the kitchen floor. He stopped near the little window and then came across the floor again.

'He's trying to find out how that ghost was handled,' Wade whispered to Cozetta. 'He'll see that trap door in a minute.'

Just at that instant, the trap door was jerked up.

'Here it is, Ma,' Tank yelled. 'A tunnel leading toward the river. Somebody's down there. You keep him from coming up here and I'll stop him from getting away at the other end of the tunnel.'

The trap door slammed shut and Wade started moving as fast as he could over the uneven floor toward the end of the tunnel. Cozetta was right behind him. At the tunnel mouth, Wade pulled aside the branches and started to step out. A shot slammed into the branches, making Wade duck back inside.

'He's found it already,' Wade said.

'He must have gotten down here just in time to see you move those branches,' Cozetta said.

'We'll have a better chance against Kate at the other end,' Wade decided. 'Tank will pick us off if we try to go out this end.'

Wade led the way back toward the house end of the tunnel. But well before they reached the trap door, a wave of smoke swept down the tunnel toward them. Wade stopped.

'Kate has thrown some burning wood through the trap door,' he exclaimed. 'She's trying to smoke us out of here.' He began backing toward the creek end of the tunnel.

'What are we going to do?' Cozetta asked,

alarm in her voice.

'I don't know,' Wade admitted. 'Maybe the smoke won't amount to much.'

But after a couple of minutes, he knew that wasn't going to be the case. Either Kate had put a lot of burning wood through the trap door, or she was feeding the fire from above, keeping the trap door closed most of the time so the smoke would roll down the tunnel.

Wade knew that they'd have to do something right away. Already Cozetta was choking on the smoke, and he had started coughing and his eyes were watering. Breathing was getting difficult.

They had to get out soon. But there was only one way out, and that was right into Tank Crudup's guns.

CHAPTER SEVENTEEN

'We're going to die if we don't get some fresh air,' Cozetta gasped.

Wade suddenly remembered the hole in the roof of the tunnel that he had covered with a rock. It he could push that rock aside, some of the smoke might go up through that hole.

The trouble with that idea was that he'd have to go back into the thicker smoke to reach the spot where the horse had broken through the roof of the tunnel. His eyes were already watering until he couldn't see much and the smoke was choking him.

'You stay here,' he gasped to Cozetta. 'I've got to go back into the tunnel.'

'You'll choke to death,' Cozetta objected.

'I'll do that here if I don't get some fresh air. You stay as close to the mouth of the tunnel as you can. Should be some fresh air coming through the tree limbs there.'

Working his way back into the smoke, Wade ran his hand along the roof, seeking the hole. The smoke was thicker here, choking him and making him gasp for breath. He couldn't take this very long.

Then his hand found the hole. Pushing his fist through the hole, he gave the rock a shove, knocking it aside. Immediately the smoke started pouring up through the hole as if it were a chimney.

Gasping and choking, Wade turned and stumbled back toward the opening. He finally dropped to his knees and crawled. He found the air fresher with less smoke along the floor of the tunnel. He was crawling along, almost blinded, when he bumped into Cozetta.

'What did you do?' Cozetta asked. 'The smoke is clearing out.'

'I remembered a hole in the roof that I'd covered,' Wade said. 'Makes a natural chimney.'

'We can stay here now till dark if we have to,' Cozetta said in relief.

Wade shook his head. 'No chance. Kate and Tank are going to see that smoke and they'll plug the hole again. Then we'll be smoked out of here like rats. We're got to find a way to get out.'

'How?' Cozetta asked. 'Kate's at one end of the tunnel and Tank's at the other.'

'It will have to be at this end,' Wade said. 'The other end is full of smoke. The only decent air we'll have will be on this side of the air hole.'

Wade moved down to the end of the tunnel and stopped just short of touching the tree limbs blocking the tunnel's mouth. Lying flat, he jerked a limb out of the mass.

As he pulled the limb inside the tunnel, the rest of the limbs shook and threatened to fall. A gun roared and a bullet slammed through the limbs. Wade wasn't surprised. Tank was on the alert.

Wade rustled the limbs again. Again the gun roared. Then after a pause, Tank's next shot whistled straight down the tunnel. Tank had moved around until he was facing the tunnel squarely.

'Keep down,' Wade called softly to Cozetta.

He rustled the limbs again and after Tank had fired, he groaned as loud as he could. He stopped rustling the limbs and groaned several times.

Cozetta crept down next to Wade. 'Did he hit you?' she cried worriedly.

Wade held up his hand for quiet. 'No,' he whispered. 'But I want him to think he did.'

Cozetta nodded understandingly. 'Do you think he'll come in to see?'

Wade groaned again then spoke softly. 'I'm banking on it. Go back a ways and lie flat. He may fill this tunnel full of lead before he risks coming to take a look.'

After another weaker groan, Wade lapsed into silence. Time dragged on for five minutes. Then suddenly Tank emptied his gun into the mouth of the tunnel. Wade knew from the sound that he had moved in much closer.

Wade kept quiet. Pulling his gun from its holster, he cocked it, keeping his eyes on the limbs blocking the mouth of the tunnel. He wondered how long it would be before Tank became convinced that Wade was out of action. Maybe he wouldn't risk looking in the tunnel at all.

The waiting was nerve-wracking. Wade began to imagine noises outside the tunnel. Still he didn't dare move. Any sound made inside the tunnel that could be heard outside would expose Wade's trickery.

Then suddenly a tree limb at the tunnel's mouth moved slightly. Wade's finger tightened on the trigger. He had to wait till he had a definite target before he began shooting.

The limb rustled again but still he waited. He hadn't seen anything move yet but that limb. Other limbs shook now, making a racket that could be heard the length of the tunnel.

Still Wade didn't move. Tank wasn't going to find out for sure about him until he looked inside. Wade had to be ready.

A rock rattled outside. Then for another agonizing minute there was no sound. Wade felt his nerves tighten until they threatened to snap. Finally, a tree limb rustled again as it was pulled aside. Tank's face appeared for just a moment.

Wade's nerves could take no more. He squeezed the trigger. Again and again he fired. Tank yelled and his face disappeared instantly. Wade scrambled to his feet and lunged to the opening. But a bullet into the tree limbs stopped him. He hadn't scored a disabling hit on Tank. Through the tree limbs he saw Tank disappearing into the water willows along the creek. He was holding one hand over his other arm but his gun was up and ready. Wade had bungled his one chance. Tank was only slightly wounded.

Wade fired the last two bullets in his gun after Tank, then ducked back and reloaded from the loops in his belt. Outside, the firing began again. Wade leaned back against the tunnel wall but he soon realized that the bullets were not penetrating the limbs covering the tunnel.

The shots outside were coming from two different places, but none of the bullets were hitting the tunnel. Then Wade heard Tank yell loudly.

'Hey, Uncle Jasper. It's me, Tank. I've got that marshal bottled up in a tunnel here. Help me smoke him out.'

More shots tore the afternoon apart. Tank yelled louder than ever, anger and frustration in his voice.

'Stop shooting, you idiot! It's Tank. Shoot at that tunnel. Tillotson is in there.'

'I know who I'm shooting at, you cattle thief!' another voice shouted from farther up the creek. Wade recognized the gravelly voice of Jasper Dovel.

'This is no time for us to be fighting,' Tank yelled. 'We've got a chance to get rid of that marshal. You've got a big reward out for him, you know.'

'You're not going to collect it,' Dovel shouted back.

The firing increased and Wade called back to Cozetta.

'Better stay here and keep down, I'm going out while Tank is busy.'

'Be careful,' Cozetta said, moving down close to Wade.

Wade checked his gun, then pushed some tree limbs aside. The firing continued by no bullets came toward the tunnel. Dodging outside, Wade dropped down behind some water willows and tried to size up the situation.

He couldn't see either combatant, but he could tell where they were by the firing. Tank was down in the water willows a little to Wade's left; Jasper Dovel was behind some rocks that had tumbled down from the low bluffs along the river bank to his right. Tank was using his revolver but Jasper had a rifle.

Tank yelled again but this time it was in pain. Jasper left his rock protection and dodged down into the willows himself, pumping more bullets in the direction of Tank. Tank fired again but his bullet obviously didn't come near his target. Wade guessed he was hit hard.

Jasper Dovel dodged closer. Tank suddenly stood up either in confusion or to get a better shot at Dovel. Dovel stopped and brought up his rifle. Before Tank could duck down, Dovel fired twice. Tank flopped backward.

Wade was looking at Tank when a bullet slapped into the bluff beside him. He flopped down, realizing that Jasper Dovel had turned the rifle on him, apparently convinced that he had put Tank out of the fight.

Wade, running low, moved out from the bluff into the bigger willows near the creek. He didn't fire at Dovel, hoping that Dovel had lost track of him.

Dovel kept firing his rifle, probing the willows for Wade. Wade moved as quietly as possible.

Limited to a revolver as Tank had been, Wade knew he had to get closer to Jasper to be effective against that rifle. He passed the spot where Tank was lying. He gave him only a glance, enough to know that Tank's fighting days were over.

Cautiously then he moved along the creek. There were no willows here on the sand, but Dovel was still shooting down into the willows where Wade had been. Running now, Wade move closer.

Suddenly there was a scream that brought Wade to a halt. He saw that Cozetta had come out of the tunnel and Kate had caught her there. Kate, apparently attracted by the shooting along the creek, had come down from the house and now she was holding Cozetta with one hand and had her gun in the other, waving it around as if undecided who to shoot at.

Then, seeing Wade standing up along the river watching her struggle with Cozetta, she fired at him. Wade ducked down as Cozetta renewed her fight with Kate. She was no match for Kate in size or weight, but she had youth on her side and she put up enough of a fight so Kate wasn't able to do much with her gun.

Wade concentrated then on Jasper Dovel. If he rushed over to help Cozetta, Dovel would pick him off like a duck sitting on a pond. Kate didn't seem to be trying to hurt Cozetta, only using her as a shield against both Wade and Jasper.

Jasper was obviously distracted by the commotion Kate had created. Even though

Kate had located Wade, Jasper had not. He fired once more where he had seen Wade last.

Wade was closer to Jasper now, but he still couldn't see him among the willows. Kate was trying to drag Cozetta up the hill to the house. If she got into the house, she could hold out there indefinitely. Wade wouldn't risk hurting Cozetta to get to her. He couldn't be sure however, what Jasper would do.

Wade found a fair-sized rock and threw it far to his right. Jasper leaped up when the rock hit and fired his rifle at the spot.

'Drop the rifle, Dovel!' Wade yelled, moving out where he had Dovel in his sights.

The old rancher wheeled, bringing his rifle around, firing as he did. The bullet went wide of its mark. Wade waited no longer. His bullet slammed into Jasper's shoulder, driving him back and making him lose his grip on the rifle.

Wade ran forward and kicked away the rifle before Jasper could reach it with his good hand. Keeping his gun trained on the rancher, he quickly searched him for a hand gun. He didn't have any.

'Kate is at the bottom of your trouble, you know,' Wade said.

Jasper scowled. 'I don't need you to tell me that.'

Wade glanced over the hill where Kate was still fighting to drag Cozetta up the hill. For a small girl, Cozetta was putting up a great battle. Wade looked back at Jasper Dovel.

Dovel couldn't give him any more trouble if Wade took his rifle.

'I don't need Kate and I don't need no marshal around here,' Dovel half shouted. 'Get out and leave me alone or I'll kill you.'

Wade picked up the rifle. 'That's pretty big talk when I've got your rifle,' he said. 'You just simmer down while I go after Kate.'

With Jasper's rifle in one hand and his own gun in the other, Wade started running through the willows toward the hill leading up to the house. At the far side of the willows, just short of the tunnel mouth, Wade dropped Jasper's rifle where he was sure the old man wouldn't find it for a while.

Kate and Cozetta were halfway to the house and Kate was in a wild rage. She fired twice at Wade but her shots were not even close. Cozetta was kicking her shins and now she got her teeth into her arm.

Wade ran harder. At any second now, Kate was going to turn her gun on Cozetta. She would have done it before this, he was sure, except she knew that once Cozetta was gone, Wade wouldn't hesitate to shoot her. Wade had never shot a woman, but he knew he would if Kate hurt Cozetta.

Kate had been gaining some ground in her struggle to get to the house, but now Cozetta was jerking back and the two women seemed to be fighting in a circle. Wade was running as hard as he could now, trying to get to Kate before she could hurt Cozetta or get in a lucky shot at him.

Cozetta, her head down, was fighting savagely, pushing the much heavier Kate around like a big sack of meal. Kate was trying to hold Cozetta and at the same time shoot at Wade.

Then suddenly Kate screamed and fell backward. Cozetta was thrown aside and she fell, too. Wade couldn't see for a moment what had happened.

Then he reached Kate and aimed a kick at her gun hand as she tried to wheel the gun around at him. Kate screamed again.

'You broke my hand!' she howled. 'And I broke an ankle.'

Wade saw then what had thrown her. She had stepped into the hole in the roof of the tunnel. Gingerly she pulled her foot out of the hole. Wade picked up her gun, keeping his own gun trained on her.

Wade glanced at Cozetta. 'You all right?'

Cozetta nodded, not trying to get up. Her face was flushed and she was gasping for air.

'You backed her into that hole on purpose, didn't you?' Wade said, looking from Cozetta to Kate.

'I thought she was never going to step in it,' Cozetta said.

'I'll get you both yet,' Kate yelled.

'I wouldn't plan on that,' Wade said. He looked at Kate sitting on the ground rubbing her ankle, then at Jasper moving slowly up the hill, holding a hand over his bleeding shoulder.

'You won't kill me,' Kate said confidently.

'That's right,' Wade said. 'But the law will have something to say about what you'll be doing for the next few years after it hears that you killed Brent Runyan.'

'She owes me for four hundred head of cattle she stole, too.' Jasper said, coming up the hill.

'You won't press any charges against me, Jasper,' Kate said.

'That's what you think!' Jasper roared. 'That sneaking son of yours tried to kill me, to boot. There won't be any more Crudups on this range.'

'But there is going to be a U.S. marshal,' Cozetta said, looking at Wade.

'Maybe,' Wade agreed. 'But only until I resign from that job.'

Jasper scowled and sighed heavily. 'I'm an old man and things are changing too fast for me. I suppose I can live with a marshal for a neighbor.'

Wade helped Cozetta to her feet, and they moved down to the edge of the bluff above the tunnel mouth. Wade jerked his head back at Kate and Jasper.

'They're not going anywhere. Jasper doesn't feel like it and Kate can't walk.'

'Are you going anywhere now that your job

here is done?' Cozetta asked.

'Don't have to, providing I'm given a good reason for staying.'

Her arms came up around his neck and she gave him the best reason he could think of.

G.K. Hall & Co.
P.O. Box 159
Thorndike, Maine 04986
USA
Tel. (800) 223-2336

All our Large Print titles are designed for easy reading, and all our books are made to last.